J. T. EDSON'S
FLOATING OUTFIT

The toughest bunch of Rebels that ever lost a war, they fought for the South, and then for Texas, as the legendary Floating Outfit of "Ole Devil" Hardin's O.D. Connected ranch.

MARK COUNTER was the best-dressed man in the West: always dressed fit-to-kill. **BELLE BOYD** was as deadly as she was beautiful, with a "Manhattan" model Colt tucked under her long skirts. **THE YSABEL KID** was Comanche fast and Texas tough. And the most famous of them all was **DUSTY FOG**, the ex-cavalryman known as the Rio Hondo Gun Wizard.

J. T. Edson has captured all the excitement and adventure of the raw frontier in this magnificent Western series. Turn the page for a complete list of Floating Outfit titles.

J.T. Edson

FROM HIDE AND HORN

CHARTER BOOKS, NEW YORK

FROM HIDE AND HORN

A Charter Book / published by arrangement with
Transworld Publishers, Ltd.

PRINTING HISTORY
Corgi edition published 1969
Berkley edition / October 1980
Charter edition / December 1987

ISBN: 1- 441-25831-X

Charter Books are published by The Berkley Publishing Group,
200 Madison Avenue, New York, New York 10016.
The name "Charter" and the "C" logo
are trademarks belonging to Charter Communications, Inc.
PRINTED IN THE UNITED STATES OF AMERICA

10 9 8 7 6 5 4 3 2 1

For Mike Muse and his box of doom,
disaster, subtle violence and sudden death.

AUTHOR'S NOTE

The events recorded in this book follow
on from those in GOODNIGHT'S DREAM
and tell how he made it come true.

FROM HIDE AND HORN
COLONEL GOODNIGHT'S TRAIL CREW

Charles Goodnight	trail boss

OD Connected — OD

Dusty Fog	segundo
Mark Counter	point rider
The Ysabel Kid	scout
Red Blaze	trail hand
Billy Jack	trail hand

Swinging G — G

"Rowdy" Lincoln	cook
"Turkey" Trott	cook's assistant
"Boiler" Benson	trail hand
Eddie Quinn	trail hand
"Spat" Bodley	trail hand
"Austin" Hoffman	trail hand
Eph Horn	horse wrangler
Ross Phares	horse wrangler
Will Trinka	night hawk

D4S — D 4 S

Dawn Sutherland	trail hand
Vern Sutherland	trail hand
Josh Narth	trail hand

Bench P — P

Tod Ames	trail hand
"Jacko" Lefors	trail hand

Lazy F   **㓵**
Solly Sodak   trail hand
"Pick" Visscher   trail hand

Double Two   **22**
Swede Ahlén   trail hand
Burle Willock   trail hand

Flying H   **⊣⊢**
Shermy Sherman   trail hand
Alex Raymar   trail hand

CHAPTER ONE
You Hire Cheap, You Get Cheap Results

Bearers of bad news are rarely welcome and the tall, lean man clad in travel-stained range clothes shuffled his feet uncomfortably as he finished his tale of misfortune and failure. Seated at his desk, Joseph Hayden glared coldly at the man.

Rooms in the small hotel at Throckmorton, Texas, did not usually offer such facilities. Nor, especially since the end of the War between the States, did they normally house guests of wealth and social prominence. So the manager had willingly complied with Hayden's requests. Small, dapperly attired to the height of current Eastern fashion, Hayden had a hardness of face and cold eyes. He invariably spoke in a clipped voice which showed an expectancy of receiving instant obedience.

"So Goodnight's managed to regather his herd, has he?" Hayden said at last.

"That's what the feller I met on the way here told me," the westerner, a typical cattle country hardcase, replied. "He allowed that Mr. Wednesbury had just got to the cabin when about thirty Swinging G cowhands jumped them. Your partner and all but one of the others went down in the fighting 'n' the feller allowed he was lucky to get away alive."

"I'll just bet he was," Hayden sniffed, having no illusions about the quality of the men his penny-pinching late partner had insisted on hiring. "Goodnight hasn't got thirty men, counting his ranch crew and the extra help he hired for the trail drive."

"He's got Cap'n Dusty Fog backing him," the man pointed out, his tone indicating that he was giving a perfect explanation for Wednesbury's defeat and death.

Maybe Hayden had never worn a uniform, and spent the war years building up a sizeable fortune, but he had heard the name mentioned by his hired man.

During the last years of the War, Dusty Fog had risen to a prominence as a military raider and fighting cavalry commander equaled only by Dixie's other two experts, Turner Ashby and John Singleton Mosby. At the head of the Company "C," Texas Light Cavalry, Dusty Fog had caused havoc, loss and despair among the Yankee Army in Arkansas. In addition to his excellent military record, he was rumored to have twice helped Belle Boyd, the Rebel Spy, to accomplish dangerous assignments.* With the War ended, he had returned to Texas and taken over as segundo of the great OD Connected ranch. Circumstances soon sent him into strife-torn Mexico on a mission of international importance, which he brought to a most satisfactory conclusion.†

In addition to his past military glories, people spoke of Dusty Fog as a tophand with cattle. They told many tales of his ambidextrous prowess, lightning-fast way of drawing a pair of 1860 Army Colts and wonderfully accurate shooting. Also frequently mentioned was his uncanny bare-handed fighting skills, which rendered bigger, heavier, stronger men helpless in his grasp.

Hayden did not know how many of the legends about

---

*Told in *The Colt and the Saber* and *The Rebel Spy*.
†Told in *The Ysabel Kid*.

Dusty Fog might be true. Nor did he particularly care. Except that Dusty Fog was Goodnight's nephew and so a factor to be reckoned with when plotting the downfall of the stocky, bearded, trail-blazing rancher from Young County.

"Is the man with you?" Hayden inquired.

"Nope," the hardcase answered. "He allowed that he wasn't staying anywheres close to Goodnight in case somebody was took alive and talked. Last I saw of him, he was headed East like the devil after a yearling." Then, feeling he ought to express his condolences, he went on, "I'm real sorry about Mr. Wednesbury, Boss."

"So am I," Hayden replied. "I'll put a mourning band on for him. What did you learn around Mineral Wells?"

"Not much at first. The Sutherland gal come in with Mark Counter and the Ysabel Kid, trying to talk some of the ranchers' wives to get up a herd and send it to Goodnight. They weren't getting any place, then Wardle, Hultze and the others got back from chasing the cattle Chisum stole. Seems like Goodnight'd offered to let them send cattle and men on his drive to Fort Summer. So's they'd have hands who knowed how to trail cattle and money enough to pay for another big drive."

"Where to?" Hayden demanded.

"I heard up to the railroad in Kansas," answered the hardcase and made a deprecatory gesture. "Only I figure somebody'd been joshing the gal who told me. Hell! They'd never take cattle right up there."

Although Hayden did not show it, he disagreed with the speaker. Conditions were sufficiently bad in Texas for men to take desperate chances in the hope of improving them. Having supported the Confederate States during the War, most people in Texas found themselves left with a worthless currency following the South's defeat. Texas had no major industries capable of competing on the national market, nor mineral assets which might help its people to return to solvency.*

---

*It would be many years before oil became a factor in the Texas economy.

All they had was cattle. The longhorns grazed in enormous herds on land capable of supporting them and many more, a potential source of wealth if they could only be sold. At first there were only the hide-and-tallow factories willing to take the cattle—at three or four dollars a head, calves thrown in free. They bought by the herd, killing, stripping off the hide and tallow, then dumping the meat and remains of the carcasses into the Brazos River.

Charles Goodnight and Oliver Loving found another market. With something like 11,000 Indians on reservations needing to be fed, the U.S. Army in New Mexico wanted all the beef they could buy. So the Texan partners had decided to make a stab at supplying that need. They had made two successful drives, pioneering a trail and learning many valuable lessons, before word of their efforts leaked out.

No cattleman, Hayden had recognized the potential source of profit offered by delivering beef to the Army. Longhorns could be bought for less than five dollars a head in Texas and sold at Fort Sumner for eight cents a pound on the hoof. With an average-sized steer—the Army wanted neither cows nor yearlings—weighing about eight hundred pounds, there would be a very fair return on his outlay.

Along with his partner, Wednesbury, Hayden had gone to Fort Sumner in the hope of obtaining contracts to supply the cattle. Although Loving had died from a wound gathered in a Comanche Indian attack, Goodnight had put in a bid to deliver three thousand steers by early July, relying on rancher John Chisum to fill the number for him. There would still have been a good opening for Hayden, but he wanted much more than that. Before him lay a vision of enormous wealth. By buying cheap from the impoverished ranchers of Texas, he hoped to make a vast fortune.

Figuring Goodnight to be a threat to that vision, Hayden had tried to remove him. With the aid of the unscrupulous Chisum, Hayden had hoped to plant eleven hundred head of stolen steers into Goodnight's shipping

herd and have their owners find them. By bad luck,
Goodnight had learned of the thefts in time and turned
the stolen cattle away. Although Hayden's men had
managed to stampede the Swinging G herd, the attempt
was only partially successful and the losses had been made
up. Determined to attend to Goodnight's ruin himself,
Wednesbury had taken some men to Young County and
died with nothing achieved. Not even the loss of the eleven
hundred head stolen by Chisum had slowed Goodnight
down, it seemed. In some way the rancher had not only
made his peace with the irate owners, but persuaded them
to make good the missing cattle.

From what Hayden remembered of Goodnight, he did
not lightly discard the idea of the alternative destination
for cattle mentioned to his hired man. Goodnight had
foresight and was aware of the crying need for beef on the
Eastern seaboard. While it would not be possible to trail
cattle that far, they could be shipped east on the
transcontinental railroad.

If the long drive could be made, Hayden saw a second,
even greater, market opened. The forts of New Mexico
were less accessible to the owners of the eastern and
southern ranches than from his present location. Kansas
would be open to all. Nor, using it, would the Army
become flooded with stock so that they could lower their
prices. If Goodnight's actions in taking along men from
his neighbors' ranches was anything to go on, he intended
that everybody would benefit from the markets he
opened.

That was the last thing in Hayden's mind. The longer
he could keep the markets to himself, the greater would be
his profits. From the money the herds brought in, he
could buy property, take over ranches from bankrupt
owners, and build himself a cattle empire.

Let Goodnight pave the way and others would follow.
So he must be stopped or, coming from a breed which did
not know the meaning of the word "beaten," killed. Let
Charles Goodnight, honored scout of Captain Jack
Cureton's famed company of Texas Rangers and master
cattleman fail, others would hesitate to try. The problem

facing Hayden was how he might best achieve his intentions.

"Can we get men down there in time to stop the Mineral Wells cattle reaching Goodnight?" Hayden asked, breaking in on his train of thought and seeking for the means to deal with the rancher.

"Not afore they get to him," the man admitted.

"Then why didn't you do something before you came here?"

"How d'you mean, boss?"

"You could have followed them and stampeded the herd."

"With Mark Counter trail bossing it and the Ysabel Kid riding scout?"

Looking blankly at his employee, Hayden saw a flicker of consternation cross the other's face. Yet Scabee had shown courage, if not initiative, on more than one occasion since they first met. Hayden wondered who Mark Counter and the Ysabel Kid might be. If he had lived for any time close to the lower reaches of the Rio Grande he would have known the answer to the latter part of the question.

Born in the village of the *Pehnane* Comanche, only son of a tough Irish-Kentuckian mustanger-cum-smuggler and his Creole-Comanche wife, the Ysabel Kid had been raised and educated among the Wasps, Quick-Stingers or Raiders—the white man's translation of *Pehnane*—band. From his maternal grandfather, Chief Long Walker of the fabled Dog Soldier war lodge, the boy had learned all those things a Comanche brave-heart must know.* He could ride any horse ever foaled and knew ways to bring a strange, hostile mount to his will. Given expert instruction in the handling of a variety of weapons, he also knew how to walk in silence through the thickest brush, follow tracks barely visible to less keen eyes, locate hidden enemies and conceal himself in minute cover. One thing he had never been taught was to nurse too great a respect for the sanctity of human life.

*Told in *Comanche*.

Fortunately for the peace of Texas, he had never made use of his knowledge in the manner of a *Pehnane* brave. However, he put much of his training to use helping his father as a smuggler or, during the War, delivering cargoes, run through the U.S. Navy's blockading squadron into Matamoros, to Confederate officials north of the Rio Grande. During that time he had gained a reputation for being one tough, very capable and deadly *hombre*. Maybe he did not rate high in the use of a revolver, but none could fault his handling of a bowie knife, or belittle his ability with a rifle. Young he might be, yet the hardcases along the bloody border grew silent and well behaved in his presence.

With the War over, the Kid had intended to resume the family trade. Bushwhack lead cut down his father and, while hunting for Sam Ysabel's killers, he had met Dusty Fog. Lone-handed smuggling held no attraction for the Kid, so, having helped Dusty complete the important mission, he accepted the other's offer of employment. Many folk slept easier in their beds knowing that the Ysabel Kid now rode on the side of justice. His talents were given to the OD Connected and utilized by the Ole Devil Hardin to help friends in trouble. It would have gone very hard for any man the Kid had found acting in a suspicious manner in the vicinity of the herd he helped to guard.

While he would quickly achieve a fame equaling that of Dusty Fog or the Ysabel Kid, at that time Mark Counter was less known than his companions. Son of a wealthy Big Bend rancher, Beau Brummel of the Confederate Cavalry, Mark was known as a tophand with cattle, something of a dandy dresser, yet immensely strong and exceptionally able in a roughhouse brawl. Less was known of his skill as a gunfighter. Nor, riding as he did in the shadow of Dusty Fog, would he ever gain his just acclaim. Yet men who were in a position and possessed knowledge of such things would say that Mark was second only to the Rio Hondo gun wizard in the matter of fast draw and accurate shooting.

Like the Kid, Mark helped Dusty on that important

assignment. Instead of returning to his father's R over C spread, he took on at the OD Connected. Not just as a hand, but to ride as part of the floating outfit, the elite of the crew. On the enormous ranches like the OD Connected, four to six men—tophands all—were employed to travel the distant ranges instead of being based on the main house. Being aware what was at stake, Ole Devil Hardin had sent his floating outfit to help Goodnight. Although Hayden did not know it, the floating outfit had been mainly responsible for the failure of his plans.

"So Goodnight will be moving out soon," Hayden commented coldly. "And with a full three thousand head."

"Sure, Boss," Scabee admitted. "Anyways, you've got our cattle on the trail by now, ain't you?"

"Yes, and with Chisum handling the drive. He knows the trail to Fort Sumner as well as Goodnight does. And he's got a good four days' start. But I don't mean to take chances. I'm going to make sure that Goodnight doesn't arrive."

"You figuring on taking men after the Swinging G herd, Boss?"

"Not me personally. I'm going after Chisum and joining him on the trail. A man who'd betray his friend won't play square with an employer. So I'm going to be with him when he reaches Fort Sumner."

"Then who——"

On his arrival at Throckmorton, Hayden had found that a suite was an unknown quantity at the hotel. Explaining his needs, he had had three ordinary rooms converted into quarters for himself and his recently departed partner. Each of their bedrooms had been connected by a door to the room in which he now sat interviewing Scabee. Suddenly the hardcase cocked his head in the direction of what had been Wednesbury's quarters and chopped off his words. Down dropped his right hand, drawing the Remington Army revolver from its holster on his gunbelt and thumbing back the hammer.

Lining the gun at the door, he glanced at his employer.

"I just heard somebody in there, Boss."

"Go and see——" Hayden commanded, but the rest of the order proved to be unnecessary.

Slowly the door opened. While the sitting room had a lamp glowing over the desk, Wednesbury's bedroom lay in darkness. Standing inside, so that only his empty hands could be seen clearly, was a shadowy figure.

"Good evening," it said.

"Oh!" grunted Hayden, recognizing the voice. "It's you!"

"It's me," admitted the newcomer. "I hope you don't mind, but I can never resist the chance to eavesdrop."

"How much have you heard?" Hayden demanded, but waved back Scabee who snarled a curse and began to move toward the bedroom.

"Almost everything your uncouth friend's said. Ask him to put the gun away. If he kills me, you'll have lost your only chance of stopping Goodnight."

"Do it, Scabee," Hayden ordered. "I know this man."

"You near on got killed, feller," Scabee growled, returning the Remington to its holster. "I like to shot you when I heard you behind the door."

"If you're no better than the others Mr. Hayden hired," the man answered, still not showing himself, "I wasn't in any great danger."

"What do you think, having eavesdropped on us?" Hayden said, ignoring Scabee's indignant muttering. "Come in."

"I'll stay where I am if you don't mind," the man told him. "The less who know me the better I like it. As to what I think, the work was amateurishly handled and badly bungled."

"Maybe you could've done better?" Scabee challenged.

For a moment the newcomer did not speak, then he said, "I'm trying to think how I could have done *worse*. Well, Mr. Hayden, have you considered my offer?"

"You're asking a high price," Hayden commented.

"As you've just found out, you hire cheap, you get

cheap results," the man told him. "My price is high because I guarantee success. If I don't produce, you don't pay me."

"Just how do you figure on taking Charlie Goodnight, fancy pants?" demanded Scabee.

"My way," the newcomer replied calmly.

"For what you're asking, I'll want to know more about your way than that," Hayden warned.

"First, you tried to stop Goodnight gathering his herd and made a complicated plan to do it. That was a mistake. You were going against him on his home ground for one thing. Instead of stopping him, you just warned him of danger. You ought to have let him get the herd well along the trail, then busted him. But the way things turned out, it's happened for the best."

"How's that?"

"Well, Mr. Hayden, due to your efforts, Goodnight is taking along cattle for five of his neighbors as well as his own——"

"And that's for the best?" Scabee sneered.

"It is," agreed the shadowy figure. "Those ranchers have their hopes raised high and are looking to a rosy future. When Goodnight fails to get through, they'll be badly disappointed. So badly that none of them will have the heart to try again, and their experiences will scare off others from trying. And you'll be able to go on buying their cattle dirt cheap, sending them to the Army in New Mexico or up to Kansas with a near monopoly on doing it."

"How did you know——?" Hayden gasped.

"I guessed, but I see that I have found your motives."

"Go on," requested the impressed Hayden.

This was a vastly different kind of man from the dull-witted, unthinking hardcases who came so cheaply and carried all their brains in their trigger fingers. The speaker in the bedroom had intelligence, drew correct conclusions and came with excellent references.

"I'll stop Goodnight reaching Fort Sumner," the man promised without a hint of boasting. "How I do it is my own concern. For what you pay me, I supply everything I need——"

"Does that include men?"

"*All* I need, Mr. Hayden," the man repeated. "You will deposit my money with Bossaert at the saloon along the street. Not until you are satisfied that I have fulfilled my end of the bargain do you authorize him to give it to me."

"Do you trust him?" Hayden inquired.

"Another saloonkeeper was asked to hold money for me, but when I went to collect, claimed he had been robbed."

"What'd you do to him?" Scabee wanted to know.

"Told him how sorry I was for his bad luck. Losing my money was only the start of it."

"How come?"

"He did quite a good night's business next day. The trouble was that three of his customers died and the rest were so sick because of his liquor that he lost all his trade and got lynched by indignant citizens," the man explained. "Yes, Mr. Hayden, I can trust Bossaert. He knows that *nobody* has ever double-crossed me without very rapidly wishing he had not."

CHAPTER TWO

I've Never Shot a Man On The Trail

"That's one right forceful and determined gal, I told you, Dusty," Mark Counter declared admiringly, nodding to where Dawn Sutherland was carrying her low-horned, double-cinched saddle toward the Swinging G corral.

"She sure is," grinned Dusty Fog, also turning his eyes in the direction of the girl.

Tall, slender, but blossoming into full womanhood, Dawn Sutherland wore a man's tartan shirt and levis pants, the turned-up cuffs of which hung outside her high-heeled riding boots in the approved cowhand fashion. On her blonde hair, cut boyishly short before her return from Mineral Wells, a white Confederate Army campaign hat's brim threw a shadow over her tanned, pretty face. About her middle was a military gunbelt with a Cooper Navy revolver in its open-topped holster. Dusty had cause to know that the gun was no mere decoration. If her free-striding walk and the way she carried the heavy saddle, with a forty-foot hard-plaited Manila rope coiled at its horn and a twin-barreled ten-gauge shotgun in the boot, was anything to go on, she was a healthy, fit and strong young woman.

"If you think that blow-up with Colonel Charlie just now was something to watch, you ought to have seen the one with her pappy when she told him she was coming," Mark chuckled. "I thought that lil gal was fixing to whup us all, tooth 'n' claw, to get her way. She'll make a hand, Dusty."

"How about the rest of them?" Dusty inquired, indicating a group of ten assorted but fairly representative cowhands hovering in the background.

"They handled the herd from Mineral Wells easy enough," Mark answered. "Which, afore you tell me, I know it's nothing to what's ahead. Swede Ahlén there," he nodded to a big, powerfully built blond man, "he's the Double 2's segundo. Hultze and the other ranchers figured they should have one foreman along. Swede's not pushy and's willing to take orders as long as he figures the man giving 'em's giving the right ones."

"Do the rest of them listen to him?"

"Most do. Bench P, Lazy F and Double 2 are all pards, but the Flying H and D4S get along all right with them. Young Vern Sutherland's a mite wild, but he'll likely grow out of it when she stops being his *big* sister. That flashy-dressed, good-looking cuss's Burle Willock from the Double 2. He's a good hand. They all are but *he* knows it."

"I'll mind it," Dusty promised.

Faced with the post of segundo, second in command to Goodnight, on the trail drive, Dusty did not regard Mark's comments as snooping or a breach of confidence. With seven men each, he would have to stay constantly alert against interspread rivalry. One of the cowhand's prime virtues, which Dusty greatly admired, was his loyalty to the brand for which he rode. Yet he must persuade the trail crew to put aside thoughts of their respective outfits and weld them into a smoothly functioning working team as quickly as possible. Only by doing so could they hope to complete the six hundred-mile journey to Fort Sumner.

So every detail Dusty could learn about the men and their relationship to each other would be of the greatest help in keeping the peace and achieving unity.

Sure the drive to Fort Sumner had been completed before, but never with such a large herd or small crew. On his previous drives, Goodnight had used at least twenty trail hands to handle a thousand to fifteen hundred head. Experience had led him to believe the number was grossly excessive. Penny-pinching did not account for the view. So many men tended to get in each other's way and caused confusion in an emergency. With that in mind, Goodnight planned to deliver three thousand, five hundred head with a crew of only eighteen trail hands, his segundo, cook, cook's louse and three horse wranglers. If his gamble paid off, a herd and crew of the same general size could complete the longer journey to Kansas with a sufficient margin of profit to make the attempt worthwhile.

Much depended on Dusty as segundo for the drive's success. Never a man to flinch from responsibility, he meant to do everything in his power to see his uncle's scheme put through.

If Dusty and Mark studied and discussed the Mineral Wells cowhands in a surreptitious manner, the return scrutiny was much more frank and open. In fact, Dusty could guess at the thoughts uppermost in the newcomers' minds. How did one reconcile the Dusty Fog of legends with the actual man. Such a reputation should go with a giant figure, capable of physically dominating any company and of commanding appearance.

Dusty Fog stood five-foot six in his high-heeled boots. While his clothes had cost good money and were those of a tophand, he contrived to give them the appearance of somebody's cast-offs. A new black Stetson, low of crown and wide-brimmed in the Texas fashion, rode on his dusty blond head. His face was handsome, if not exceptionally so. If one chose to look closer, the cool grey eyes and strength of his features told the tale of the real man within. Around his waist was a finely-built gunbelt with a silver Confederate States Army buckle. Its carefully designed cross-draw holsters supported two bone-handled 1860

Army Colts. Efficient outfit though it might be, the gunbelt did nothing to lessen the small Texan's insignificant appearance—in times of peace.

If Dusty Fog failed to look the part, Mark Counter might have posed for a painting of the popular conception of a hero. Six-foot three in height, his golden blond, curly hair and almost classically handsome features topped a truly splendid physical development. A great spread of shoulders tapered down to a slender waist and long, powerfully muscled legs. Decorated with a silver concha-studded band, his costly white Stetson hinted at his affluence. Around his throat was knotted a tight-rolled green silk bandana. His broadcloth shirt—its sleeves hinting at the enormous biceps under them—and levis pants had obviously been tailored to his fit, while his boots were the best money could buy. Like Dusty, he wore a gunbelt made by a master craftsman and supporting matched ivory-handled Army Colts of Best Citizens Finish in the contoured holsters.

Over the years Dusty had grown used to the surprise people showed when meeting him for the first time. He reckoned he could win over the newly arrived cowhands and effectively deal with objections to one of his stature giving orders to larger, more imposing men.

There was, however, one disturbing element. It had been Dawn Sutherland who brought Goodnight the first warning of the stolen cattle and received an account of his dream to rebuild Texas' war-shattered economy. The idea had been that she should return to her home near Mineral Wells and persuade the local ranchers to send men and cattle to accompany the Swinging G herd. However, Dawn planned to do more than act as messenger, then sit passively in a corner while the men folk went off. Oldest child, she was aware of her responsibilities. A riding accident had lamed her father and he might never recover sufficiently to make extended journeys. Regarding her younger brother as a mere child—he lacked two years of her nineteen—she decided that it fell upon her to go on the drive and learn how to handle a trail herd. Despite arguments, pleadings by her mother, objections from her father and brother and warnings of the difficulties her presence might cause to the male trail hands, she had remained adamant. In the end, to Vern's protests, her parents had given permission for Dawn to go. Nor had Goodnight been any more successful in dissuading her.

Dawn's presence might raise problems. A good-looking girl could easily stir up the unruly, lusty younger element of the crew. However, from what he had seen, she knew how to take care of herself and steer clear of romantic troubles. It was still, however, something more added to Dusty's burden at a time when he could have done with things taken off, not added.

There had been only one incident of note on Mark's visit to Mineral Wells. Two days before the return journey was begun, he and the Kid had recognized a man whom they had last seen as part of Chisum's trail crew, with the stolen cattle. On learning that the man had been asking questions about their presence in town, they had discussed what should be done. Discarding his companion's simple, if drastic, solution, Mark had decided on keeping the man under surveillance. So the Kid had followed him when he left town and did not return in time to assist on the short drive to Young County.

While Dusty approved of Mark's decision, being interested to know if the death of Wednesbury had ended the threat to the drive, the kid's absence deprived them of his services as a scout. He would catch up to them on the trail, having collected a relay of horses from D4S before setting out after the snooper, and, fortunately, the need for his presence would be less during the earlier days of the journey.

A stirring and change of the Mineral Wells men's point of interest diverted Dusty from his thoughts. The cowhands were looking to where their trail boss had left the main house and stood on the edge of its porch with a sheaf of papers in his hand.

Charles Goodnight had the build of a Comanche warrior, middle-sized, stocky, powerfully framed but far from clumsy. Apart from his neatly trimmed beard, his face held some of that savage nation's qualities in its keen, hard eyes and impassive strength. He dressed little differently from the cowhands, except that his vest was made from the rosette-spotted hide of a jaguar which had foolishly strayed north and tried to live off his cattle. Matched rosewood handled Army Colts rode in the holsters of his gunbelt and he knew how to use them.

"The Kid's not back yet?" Goodnight inquired as his nephew and Mark walked across to join him.

"No, sir," Dusty replied. "He'll follow that feller and see who he meets if it can be done. Then he'll come back and catch up with us on the trail."

"We shouldn't need him for a week at least," the rancher said. "And I'm like you, I'd like to know if Wednesbury's partner is still in the game. Get the hands to come here, Dustine."

"Yo!" Dusty gave the old cavalry response to an order.

Sensing what was in the air, big Swede Ahlén led the other men up before Dusty had time to speak. Forming into a rough half circle before the porch, they waited eagerly to hear what Goodnight had to say.

"I'd best make a few things clear to you," the rancher announced. "You've handled herds and know what it's all about. Well. This drive'll be much the same—except that it's longer and with more cattle than you've ever tried. There's only one way we'll get through. By working together and obeying orders. I've made out these Articles of Agreement which I want you to read and sign. They'll be binding from the moment you put on your signature until the drive's over. Binding to you and just as completely to me."

"Would you read 'em out to us, Colonel Charlie?" Ahlén requested, his voice as Texan as any of the cowhands'. "Some of us're a mite shy on schooling."

Nodding soberly, the rancher complied. Maybe Goodnight had never served in the Army, or risen to higher rank than sergeant with the Texas Rangers—his title being honorary, granted in respect for his courage, integrity and qualities of leadership*—but he had a strong sense of responsibility to the men he hired. On his previous drives, he had established a code of conduct for boss and crew, setting it down in writing that all might know exactly where they stood.

In a clear voice Goodnight began to read the various paragraphs of the Articles. First he stated, in plain terms all could follow, what he as trail boss undertook to do. Then he went on to stress the importance of instant obedience to the orders of himself or his aides, Dusty Fog as segundo, or Mark Counter in the small Texan's absence. While reading the duties of the trail hands, Goodnight watched the Mineral Wells men. Nods of agreement with the various points came from the older, steadier listeners, showing that they at least accepted the Articles as satisfactory. All saw the need for the ruling that hard liquor would only be carried in the chuckwagon and used for medicinal purposes; a drunken cowhand being a danger to himself and menace to the safety of the whole drive.

At last Goodnight stopped reading. Yet something in his attitude warned the listeners that he was not finished. Whatever came next must be real important. So they waited in silence and he continued, but with a grimmer emphasis.

"If any member of the crew kills another, he will be tried by his companions and, if found guilty of murder, hung on the spot——"

"*Hung!*" repeated Burle Willock, the word bursting out in a startled pop.

"I've never shot a man on the trail," the rancher replied.

Being aware of the stresses and strains to which a trail crew found themselves subjected, Goodnight had found the last article a stout deterrent to trouble. The threat of hanging carried a grim finality which went far beyond that of being shot. Only criminals, murderers, horse or cow thieves and the like were hanged. It was a death of

---

*Dusty Fog's youth prevented him from qualifying for the title "Colonel."

disgrace. So the men would be inclined to think twice and decide wisely, Goodnight hoped, when they knew the fate awaiting them if they broke the article.

"Any man who doesn't agree with the articles needn't sign them," Goodnight said after the rumble of comment at the last article had died away. "But if he doesn't, he'll not be coming on the drive."

"They're fair enough for me, Colonel," Ahlén declared and walked forward.

"By cracky, I'm on," announced Dawn's tall, gangling, towheaded younger brother crowding up on the big blond's heels.

Man after man followed, each writing his signature or making his mark on the master copy and his own sheet of the Articles. Even Dawn signed, calmly ignoring the rancher's cold-eyed disapproval and oblivious of his attempts to will her into a change of heart.

Helping his uncle take the signatures, Dusty became aware of a commotion at the bunkhouse. Shouts, curses, crashes and other sounds of a struggle preceded the appearance through the door of a fighting pair of cowhands. Locked together, they crashed to the ground and rolled over, flailing punches at each other. Recognizing the men as Spat Bodley and Austin Hoffman, two of the Swinging G's detachment on the drive, Dusty could guess at the cause of the trouble.

Before Dusty could make a move to intervene, while Mark raced toward the fighters, a peacemaker came on the scene. Long experience had taught Rowdy Lincoln how to deal with such disturbances. So the well-padded, big, jovial-faced cook emerged carrying a large bucket which he upended over the struggling pair. The arrival of the cold, dirty water shocked the breath from the cowhands and caused them to release their grasps as they knelt facing each other. Giving them no time to recover, Mark swooped down on them. Taking hold of each cowhand by the scruff of his neck, the blond giant hoisted them erect and hurled them apart.

"Quit it!" Mark growled, looming ominously between them.

Even a hothead like young Austin Hoffman had sense enough to know when to surrender. Anybody who could pick up two grown men and toss them aside with such ease deserved to have his wishes respected. No less astute, Spat stood breathing heavily and glaring at his opponent.

Coming up on the run, Dusty went by the Mineral Wells men and halted at Mark's side to ask, "What started it?"

"Hell!" Austin sniffed indignantly. "Spat there can't take a joke."

"Some damned joke——" Spat growled. "And if you——"

"Tell it, Rowdy!" Dusty snapped, glaring the cowhand to silence.

"Boys were talking about the drive, and Austin said something about how lucky they was to have Spat along, him being such a tophand at fetching help. That was when Spat jumped him."

Annoyance bit at Dusty and he prepared to stamp out a potential cause of further trouble on the drive. Spat Bodley was an amiable man, most times, and a skilled trail hand. The comment which had goaded him to violence referred to his having twice been sent to collect help for companions in trouble. On the first occasion he had returned just too late to prevent Oliver Loving receiving a fatal wound. The second time, he had brought help just in time to save Dusty's life.

Since Loving's death, Spat had grown increasingly touchy about mentions of his part in the affair and reacted with growing hostility to talk of his fetching help. For the first time, his objections had reached the point of physical violence. Dusty wanted to avoid any repetition. There were not enough trained trail hands on the drive for him to leave either man behind; and that, while the easy way out, would not solve Spat's problem. So Dusty thought fast and put his decision into words.

"Go and clean out the barn, Spat!"

Normally such a menial task would have been performed by the horse-wranglers. Knowing why he had been given it, Spat went without another word. Dusty

turned cold eyes to a slightly defiant Austin, but
addressed his next words to the cook.

"You were saying that new backhouse hole wants to go
down deeper, Rowdy?"

"It could do with a couple of foot deeper, cap'n,"
Lincoln admitted.

"Take Austin here and he'll do it for you."

Shock twisted at the cowhand's face and he gasped,
"Me! On the blister end of a shovel. I'll be damned——"

"I'm telling you to do it!" Dusty cut in coldly. "It's that,
or go ask for your time."

Knowing that Goodnight would support his nephew's
statement, Austin made a fast decision. Work was not
easy to find in Texas, especially highly paid work like
trail-driving, and riding for the Swinging G carried a
certain significance. It meant such a man was a cowhand
of high quality. Folks would think twice before hiring a
feller whom Colonel Goodnight had fired.

Nor did Austin discount Dusty's own part in the
matter. Unlike the Mineral Wells men, he had come to
know the small Texan very well. Not only had Dusty
demonstrated his strange, uncanny almost, bare-hand
fighting skill, but two days earlier had been captured by a
pair of Wednesbury's men and escaped. Even having his
hands bound behind his back had not prevented Dusty
from gaining his freedom, killing one of his captors and
taking the second prisoner. So Austin figured that Dusty
Fog did not need the backing of any man to enforce his
intentions.

"I hates digging," Austin said, trying to carry off the
affair in a light manner. "But I hates work-hunting worse.
Lead me to it, Rowdy, and watch me make like a gopher."

"Have you any work needs doing, Rowdy?" Dusty
asked before the cook left.

"Just a few things to load on the bed-wagon is all,
cap'n."

"Take three of these fellers to help you," Dusty
ordered, indicating the onlookers. "Swede, have half of
them that's left to help the wranglers. Mark, take the rest
to spell Uncle Charlie's men on the herd until nightfall."

"Yo!" answered Ahlén and Mark echoed the word, then they turned to give their orders. Mark included Dawn in his party, for she was to be classed as an ordinary hand and take her share of the work.

That evening the whole trail crew were gathered for supper when Austin came into the cookshack. No cowhand took kindly to digging and the youngster scowled unpleasantly around. Watching the expression on Austin's face, Dusty prepared to ram home the point he wanted to make.

"Do you know why I made you do it?" Dusty asked, making sure his words carried to all the men.

"For starting that fuss," Austin guessed.

"That was only a lil part of it. I figured you should learn how it feels to be made do something you hate doing. That's what happened to Spat, with Oliver Loving and again with me. He didn't leave either time because he was scared, but because he was ordered to do it. Spat hated like hell having to obey—and it was a damned sight harder thing to do than dig a backhouse hole. But he's a good hand and he knows that orders have to be obeyed. So he did what he was told. And each time, he turned right round then came back after he'd done what he was sent to do."

"I never thought——" Austin began.

"You should try it some time," Dusty told him. "It's easier on the hands than riding the blister end of a shovel. And the rest of you can get this. Spat's full capable of standing up for hisself, but I don't aim to have him doing it on this drive. The next man to mention it, even as a joke, I'll fire and run off without pay; even if it happens while we're driving through the gates of Fort Sumner."

"Reckon he'd be mean enough to try it, Boiler?" Burle Willock asked the grizzled Swinging G cowhand seated at his side.

"You'd best believe he'd *do* it," the old-timer grunted and rose to walk away.

"He talks big, don't he, Jacko?" Willock grinned to one of his cronies. "Only I noticed that he let Mark Counter stop that fight."

"Leave us not forget he's Colonel Charlie's nephew," Jacko Lefors warned.

"Likely *he'll* not let us forget *that*," Willock replied. "Thing being, how'll he stack up on his own. Could be we'll find out afore this here drive's through, Jacko boy."

CHAPTER THREE

It's Just Part of Growing Up

Although the sun had barely peeped above the eastern horizon, Dawn left the Swinging G ranch house accompanied by Mark and Dusty's cousin, Red Blaze. A tall, well-built young man, Red had a fiery thatch of hair, a pugnaciously handsome face and sported a bandana of such a violent clash of colors that he might have been color-blind. He wore range clothes of good cut and twin walnut-handled Army Colts hung butt forward in low cavalry-twist-draw holsters. One of the floating outfit, and Dusty's second-in-command during the War, he had a name for hotheaded, reckless courage and a penchant for becoming involved in more than his fair share of fights. So much so that few people recognized his virtues. Dusty knew him to be steady enough when giving a job of work and willingly trusted him to carry out any task he received.

Maybe the hour was early, but Vern Sutherland was already sitting on his *tobiano* gelding, a black horse with three clearly defined patches of white on its body.

"Come on!" the youngster greeted enthusiastically. "Time's a-wasting. Let's get moving."

A hot flush crept to Dawn's cheeks and she snapped, "Climb down and stop acting *loco*."

"Yah!" Vern answered hotly. "I don't know why you had to come along!"

"Because I figured we should have somebody in the family who knows about trailing cattle, that's why!" Dawn told him.

"What about me, huh?" Vern blazed. "I'm——"

"You pair want to wake up Colonel Charlie 'n' Dusty?" Mark put in.

"Well look at him!" Dawn snorted, knowing the two men were awake and already preparing to leave for the herd. "Acting like a kid going on a Sunday School picnic for the first time."

Ignoring the comment, Vern grinned at the two cowhands. "What say we——"

"Have you fed yet?" Mark interrupted.

"Ain't hungry!" Vern replied.

"You will be comes nightfall," the big blond stated. "Go and eat, we're just headed there."

"Sure, Mark," Vern said, reining his horse around and sending it running toward the cookshack. Just before he reached the wall he turned the *tobiano* in a rump-scraping swing and rode back to halt before the trio. "How about that?"

"Not bad," Red Blaze commented dryly. "Trouble being, you'll tucker the hoss out afore we get to the herd."

"Nah!" Vern scoffed. "Ole Toby here eats work. He'll be running when the rest're worn down to their hocks."

"Fool kid!" Dawn snorted as her brother turned and galloped back to the cookshack. "Don't pay him no never mind. He's just trying to make out he's a man."

"We all start out that way," Mark assured her and looked pointedly at Red. "Only some of us stay like it."

"Don't you pair get at it again," Dawn groaned, for their bickering had kept her entertained the previous evening. Then she became serious. "Mark, Red, will you do something for me?"

"If we can," Red promised.

"Help me set Vern right."

"How do you mean?" Mark inquired.

"You've just seen how he acts——" Dawn began.

"It's harmless enough," Mark said tolerantly. "We're all excited. This's a big thing we're starting out to do."

"Yes, but——" the girl started.

"Now listen, Dawn gal," Mark interrupted her. "Your pappy asked me what I thought about having Vern along, and I said I reckoned he'd make a hand. I didn't say it just to please Vern—or rile you. I meant what I said. If your pappy's leg doesn't get better, young Vern'll have to grow up fast; and I reckon going on this drive'll make him."

"He's a fool kid——" Red continued.

"He's only young——" Dawn corrected hotly, bristling indignation.

"Now me," grinned Red. "I thought *you* was the one worrying about *that*."

"And anyways," Mark went on, "give him time. He'll likely grow out of it. Like I said, most of us do in the end."

"You men always stick together," Dawn sniffed, her good humor restored.

"We have to," Red explained. "It's the only way we can keep half-ways ahead of getting trampled underfoot by you women."

"Vern's not wild," Dawn stated as they drew near the cookshack. "And all that talk he gives about whooping it up in saloons's just talk. He's not been around them anywhere nears as much as he'd have you think. Fact being, he's only snuck in a couple of times when he's been sure pappy wasn't around."

"It's just part of growing up," Mark replied. "And when you get to Vern's age, you don't want a bossy sister only a year older 'n' you trying to run your life."

"I'm near on *two* years older!"

"Sure. But try to forget it. The more you ride him, the harder he'll set on showing the rest of us fellers that you're wrong."

"Mark's right on that," Red informed the girl. "I've got

two older *brothers* and I didn't cotton to them trying to run things."

"I'll mind what you say," Dawn promised and they walked into the building.

All the men present were eating heartily and appeared to be in the best of spirits. Seated near the door, tall lanky mournful Billy Jack of the OD Connected predicted all kinds of doom and disaster. Nobody took any notice of him, knowing it to be a sign that he felt all was well in the world. Under that dolorous exterior lay a bone-tough fighting man and skilled cowhand. One of the floating outfit, Billy Jack had been Dusty's sergeant major in the War and appearances in his case were very deceptive.

With the meal over, the trail crew headed for the corral. Ropes swished and hooley-ann loops* sailed through the air to drop about the necks of the horses selected for use while moving the herd out. In very quick time, every hand had caught and saddled his horse, the hooley-ann being a roping throw designed to allow several of the crew to operate at the same time around the corral. One of the first ready was Dawn, snaking her *bayo-tigre* gelding from the milling crush and throwing on its rig with practiced speed.

Already Dusty and Goodnight were riding toward the herd. Studying the steers with experienced eyes, the rancher sought for signs of restlessness. Despite the addition of the Mineral Wells stock, the assembled Swinging G animals seemed quiet enough. Goodnight's foreman, John Poe, who would be staying in Young County to gather cattle for another drive, rode up. He told his boss that the night had been quiet and uneventful, apart from the inevitable attempts by some of the wilder cattle to regain their freedom.

"You can expect that from the sort of *ladinos* we've been hauling out of the thorn-brush," the rancher said.

"Sure," Poe grinned. "Way some of 'em act, you'd figure they didn't want to go and feed up all them hungry

---

*Described in *Trail Boss*.

Apaches in New Mexico. Anyways, none of them got away."

"I didn't think they would." Goodnight replied, flashing a rare smile at his segundo and foreman. "Here's my crew. We'll move out straight away, Dustine."

"Yo!" answered Dusty, and rode to meet the approaching party.

For a long moment Goodnight sat silent, then he sucked in a deep breath. This was the start of what might easily be the salvation of Texas, or a fiasco. Whichever way it turned out, he felt it was well worth the try. Turning to Poe, the rancher offered his hand.

"I'll see you when I get back, John."

"Everything'll be ready for you, Charlie," Poe replied as they shook hands. "Good luck."

"Likely we'll need it," Goodnight said.

"All right!" Dusty said to the trail crew. "Head 'em up. Let's move 'em!"

"Yeeah!" Vern whooped, wriggling on his saddle in excitement and eagerness.

"I said move 'em, not spook 'em!" Dusty barked. "Hold it down and save that whooping for when we hit Fort Sumner."

"Sure, Cap'n Dusty," the youngster answered, face flushing with shame at the public rebuke. "I——"

"You heard," Mark growled in Vern's ear. "Get to it."

Much as Dusty would have liked to make up for the sting of his words, the chance did not arise. Along with the other hands, Vern rode to his position and made ready to start. When setting out the order in which the hands would work that day, Dusty had allocated Dawn to the swing, the forward third of the herd. Approaching her place, the girl became aware for the first time of just how many three thousand head of longhorns amounted to. She had seen gathers almost as large, during communal roundups, but nobody had ever thought of moving so many from place to place.

The range ahead seemed blanketed with steers of almost every imaginable animal coloration. While every bit as much creatures of a herd as buffalo or pronghorn antelope, the Texas longhorn showed none of their uniformity of appearance. No two steers in that vast gathering looked completely alike. Apart from the occasional muley, however, they all had one thing in common, a set of spreading, powerful and needlesharp horns.

Not that Dawn found time to sit in awed contemplation. Already the men were riding toward the cattle, gently urging them to move. Slowly, yet surely, the tremendous collection of steers started to walk in a westerly direction. At the point, Mark Counter and Swede Ahlén closed in on either side of the first steer ready to turn it anyway the trail boss signaled.

Commencing the first day's drive was always a trying time for the trail crew. So far the steers had not settled into a cohesive traveling unit. The Swinging G stock were still unsettled by the arrival of the Mineral Wells herd not thirty-six hours back. Due to the way they had been collected,* a number of Goodnight's contingent were *ladinos*, outlaws long used to free-ranging in the thorn-brush country. Given time, they might have become accustomed to herd life. Unfortunately, time was a commodity in very short supply if they were to reach Fort Sumner by the end of June. The drive had to be got on its way.

To an unknowing onlooker, everything might have seemed to be in wild confusion. There were steers which objected to being moved from such easy grazing, or *ladinos* striving to return to their wild existence, demanding attention and keeping the trail hands fully occupied.

Horses spurted, twisted, pivoted and galloped into a mucksweat, cutting off would-be bunch-quitters and turning the departing steers back into the marching column. After the resting mass had been converted into a mobile line, there was a continuous changing of positions. The better travelers shoved their way by the slower, less fit, or plain lazy remainder. Already some of the steers,

*Told in *Goodnight's Dream*.

particularly those from the Mineral Wells area, had teamed up with "traveling partners." Finding themselves separated, the partners would shatter the air with their bawling and try to balk against moving forward until reunited. They added to the confusion, as did the "lone wolves." These steers appeared to have only one aim in life, to amble up as far as the point, cut across before the leading animals, make their way down the other flank to the drag and repeat the circle. More than one cowhand started to chase a "lone wolf," thinking it was trying to escape, and retired cursing on discovering its harmless purpose.

Yet the drive continued. Following the cattle came the remuda, available for when a hand wanted a fresh horse from his work-mount.* Bringing up the rear were the chuck and bedwagons, driven by Rowdy Lincoln and his tall, lanky, freckle-faced and excitable louse, Turkey Trott. Toward evening they would speed up their teams, pass along the side of the drive, find a suitable camping ground and prepare a hot meal—the first since break-fast—for the crew.

Throughout the day Dusty and Goodnight seemed to be everywhere. Sometimes at the point, then among the swing or flank men, or back with the drag, either the rancher or the segundo would materialize wherever he was needed most.

Two hours after moving the herd off its bedground, Dusty heard a sound that called for investigation. Two steers faced each other in menacing attitudes among the bushes to the flank of the herd. Pawing up dirt, throwing back their heads and cutting loose with as masculine bawls as their castrated condition allowed, they prepared for hostilities. It was a situation which demanded an instant attention on the part of the nearest trail hand. Like some human beings, longhorns could not resist the temptation to watch a good fight. So other steers would attempt to quit the herd as spectators.

Yet stopping the contestants would not be without

*Texans did not use the word "string" for their workhorses.

risks, as Burle Willock well knew. When one of the fighting steers decided to quit, it would not linger. Twirling around, it would leave like a bat out of hell, giving all its attention to its rival and oblivious of anything ahead. Only by such tactics could the loser hope to protect its vulnerable, unprotected rear from a severe goring by the victor. Not even a cutting horse—most agile of the equine breed—could equal the turn-and-go prowess of a longhorn under those conditions. Nor did the flight necessarily follow a fight. Should one of the steers be bluffed out by the other's aggressive mien, it would take just as drastic evasion measures.

So Willock hesitated before going in too close to the animals. Not so Dusty Fog. Charging up, he made straight for the steers. Dusty sat a buckskin gelding, noted through the Rio Hondo country for its cattle-savvy, and it knew just what to do. Ignoring the chance of a fear-inspired charge, the horse rushed forward, slammed a shoulder into the nearest steer and knocked it staggering. Seeing its rival at a disadvantage, the second steer attacked. Letting out a squeal, the buckskin's victim fled for the safety of the herd.

"Stop it!" Dusty roared, guiding his horse after the triumphant assailant.

While Willock chased and turned the fleeing steer, preventing it from rushing among the other cattle, Dusty caught up with the victor. Knowing only rough treatment would calm the beast, Dusty rode alongside its rump. By catching and jerking at the steer's tail, he caused it to lose its balance and crash to the ground. On rising, as was mostly the case after a good "tailing down," the steer forgot all its antisocial notions and went quietly into the moving line.

Shortly before noon, Vern Sutherland pushed his *tobiano* down a draw after three steers which had escaped. In a foolhardy attempt to show how good a horse he rode, he had not changed mounts since starting out. While the *tobiano* overtook the steers and swung them back in the direction of the herd, it was tired.

Hearing a low snort to his left, Vern turned his head

and saw a big black *ladino* coming toward him.
Everything about the animal showed its mean nature and
it clearly aimed to fight its way to freedom. The *tobiano*
faced the steer, but Vern knew it was too leg-weary to deal
with such a dangerous proposition. For all that, the
youngster sat his ground. While he carried a holstered
Colt and knew how to use it, he made no attempt to do so.
The sound of a shot might easily cause the herd to
stampede.

On his way to the drag, Goodnight saw the youngster's
predicament and raced his *bayo-cebrunos** gelding to the
rescue. Unshipping the rope, with one end ready-tied to
the saddlehorn, he shook out its loop and gauged the
distance with his eye. The rancher approached from the
side of the steer as it began its charge. Rising to stand in
his stirrups, as a means of making a more accurate throw,
Goodnight sent the rope curling through the air. As the
loop fell and tightened about the steer's neck, the rancher
cued the *bayo-cebrunos* with his knees and brought it to a
turning halt. Manila twanged taut between longhorn and
saddlehorn. Fixing to keep anything he roped, the Texan
always tied his lariat securely to the horn and relied upon
his saddle's double girths to hold all firm. Braced ready
for the impact, the *bayo-cebrunos* kept its feet. Not so the
steer. Stopped unexpectedly with its feet off the ground,
its legs shot sideways and it slammed down hard on its
flank.

"Get them others back to the herd!" Goodnight called
to Vern. "Then go pick a fresh hoss from the remuda."

"Yo!" the youngster answered and turned to obey.

There were other incidents calling for Dusty's or
Goodnight's attention. In the late afternoon, they
combined to help Dawn deal with a group of extradeter-
mined *ladinos* which broke away. Only the girl's deft
riding ability held the bunch together long enough for the
men to reach her. She felt no shame at needing the
assistance. Not even the most experienced tophand
cowboy could have handled the steers alone.

* *Bayo-cebrunos*: a dun color, shading into smoky grey.

"Good work, Dawn," the rancher said.

"Real good," Dusty echoed, and grinned at the girl's dirt-smudged features. "And as a reward, you can take first spell on the night herd."

"How can you stand being so good to me?" Dawn yelled at the small Texan's departing back. Then she gave a resigned sigh. "It could be worse, I might have been on the middle watch."

CHAPTER FOUR

We'll Never Beat Him to Sumner

Knowing the importance of getting longhorns off their home ranges as a means of quietening them down, Goodnight had insisted that the herd be pushed hard all day. When he called a halt toward sundown, they were some fifteen miles from their starting point. After leaving the Swinging G's holding area, none of the trail hands had dismounted for longer than it took to transfer a saddle to a fresh horse, or relieve the needs of nature. At midday, Rowdy had taken the chuck wagon forward and handed out cold food to the crew as they rode by, so that they could eat but still stay on the move.

Even with the herd watered and brought to a stop in the open area selected by Goodnight for the night's bed ground, only Mark, Dawn and two of the hands rode back to where the cook had set up camp. Until the four—first part of the night guard—had eaten a meal, set out their bed rolls and returned, the remainder of the hands continued to circle the herd and quieten any restless urges the hard-driven steers still felt. Later, when the cattle were broken to the trail, there would normally only be two riders at a time on night guard. Until then, and in periods of necessity later, the number would be doubled.

When the quartet arrived to take over, the rest of the crew trooped gratefully to the camp. Dusty went with them, but Goodnight stayed by the herd to make sure the guard knew their duties. First caring for their mounts, the trail hands took and picketed their night horses ready for instant use if the need arose. With that done, they made their way to the big main fire. There Rowdy or Turkey supplied each man with a plate generously loaded with thick, savoury stew and cups of coffee in which a spoon would almost stand erect.

Little was said until the plates had been cleaned and hunger satisfied. Then the hum of conversation arose.

"How do you like being on the trail, Vern boy?" demanded Willock in a condescending manner, winking at his crony, Jacko.

"It's great!" the youngster answered enthusiastically, although he did not particularly care for the swaggering Double Two cowhand. Then, realizing that he sounded too eager for a man of the world, he tried to adopt a more nonchalant tone. "It's about what I figured it'd be."

"Is, huh?" Willock sneered, flashing a superior grin around the circle of watching and listening men. "It gets sorta rough though. Unless you've got the boss on hand to save you from them mean old steers."

"Yeah?" Vern flashed back, cheeks reddening at the sniggers which rose from Willock's friends. "Well I didn't see you doing so all-fired much about them two steers that was fighting—until Cap'n Dusty come and split 'em out for you."

A low chuckle of laughter rose at the response, coming from the men less close to Willock. Annoyance twisted at the flashy cowhand's face and he lurched to his feet.

"If you'd done more working and less sitting watching, us *men*'d've had a heap less work to do!" Willock snarled, looking mean and hooking his right thumb into his gunbelt close to the butt of the low-hanging Army Colt. "I don't take much to carrying——"

Watching the incident, Dusty scented potential trouble. Across the fire, the D4S's third member, a dour, middle-aged man called Josh Narth stirred slightly as he squat on his heels. No swaggering trouble-causer, Narth had been a long time with the Sutherland family and could be counted on to side with his boss's son. So Dusty set about nipping the discord in the bud.

"All right, you pair," Dusty said in a carrying voice as Vern also rose. "Let it drop."

"What's up?" Willock asked, looking to where Dusty heel-squat cradling a coffee cup. "Don't you reckon the hen-wrangler there can take a bit of funning?"

"He can take it, and hand it back," Dusty replied. "Only it's starting to look and sound like *you* can't take what he gives."

"Hell!" Willock spat. "We've been car——"

"The young'n' did all right today," Red Blaze remarked. "He didn't need any carrying, what I saw of him."

"Shy out of it, Red," Dusty ordered, but noticed that most of the hands muttered agreement with his cousin's statement.

"Yeah, Red!" Willock went on viciously. "Shy out. Unless you figure this D4S bunch can't——"

"That's another thing!" Dusty interrupted and gave Red a glare which prevented him from rising and carrying the matter further. "From now on I don't want to hear any more talk about the D4S, Double Two, Bench P or any other damned kind of bunch. This drive's going to be hard enough with us all pulling together. So you can forget about riding for some spread or other back to home. From here to Fort Sumner we all belong to *this* outfit."

"Them your orders," Burle asked, "or Colonel Charlies?"

A low rumble of sound came from Swede Ahlén's throat, but he said nothing. Maybe he was segundo at the Double Two, but on the trail drive he rated as an ordinary hand. So he sat back and waited to see how Dusty meant to deal with the cowhand's insolence.

"Feller, you're——" Red began, again making as if to stand up.

"Stay put, Cousin Red," Dusty ordered.

"Sure, *Cousin* Red," Willock sneered. "Leave us not forget that frying-size there's got a right pretty sister along——"

Whatever else the cowhand intended to say was never uttered. Tossing the dregs of his coffee into the fire, Dusty put down the cup and came to his feet.

"All right," he said, in the soft tone which every OD Connected cowhand came to know so well. "I figured that sooner or later I'd have to prove to somebody how I got this segundo chore for more'n just being Colonel Charlie's nephew. So tonight looks as good a time as any to do it."

As Red or Billy Jack could have warned Willock, if they had been so inclined, there were stormy times ahead of him. When Dusty's voice took on that gentle, almost caressing note, it was long gone time to hunt for the cyclone shelter. Willock did not have their knowledge of the small Texan's ways, but did have his own reputation for toughness to consider. So he stamped in gaily where angels—or as near angels as any member of the OD Connected could be—feared to tread.

"So what's that supposed to mean?" Willock demanded truculently.

"Way I see it," Dusty replied. "You figure to be wild, woolly, full of fleas and never curried below the knees. So I'm fixing to give you a chance to prove it. Guns, or bare hands. Whichever way you want."

That placed the issue as straight as anyone could ask for. Looking around, Willock read eager expectancy on the faces of the other Mineral Wells men. No hint of concern for their segundo's safety showed from the two OD Connected riders, only complete confidence in Dusty's ability to handle Willock's play no matter how he made it. That, and mocking pity at the cowhand for his stupidity. Even as Willock watched, Billy Jack turned and addressed Ahlén.

"How do you stand on this, Swede?"

"He roped the hoss," Ahlén replied immediately. "Let him ride it."

Along with the other newcomers, Ahlén recognized some of Dusty's potential, but wondered if all the stories heard about his fighting prowess were true. While none of them felt inclined to make the experiment personally, the Mineral Wells crowd were not averse to watching Willock give it a try.

Slowly Dusty began to walk around the fire. Watching the other coming his way, Willock became aware of a strange change taking place. Suddenly he found that he faced a real *big* man, not an insignificant nobody who held post as segundo by virtue of being Goodnight's nephew. In some way, Dusty gave the impression of having taken on size and heft until he towered over the biggest of the crew.

"If the button can't——" Willock commenced, hoping to turn the fight to the less dangerous Vern Sutherland.

"Vern's not in it any more." Dusty warned him, continuing to advance. "It's between you and me."

Fear bit at Willock as the small Texan delivered the ultimatum. The cowhand became increasingly aware that his salty reputation was strictly local and did not extend beyond his home ranges. Dusty Fog's name was statewide and, as Willock now realized, had been well deserved. So Willock wondered how he could back down, avoid the clash, without being laughed off the drive. There was no halfway about it. Either he ate crow or took a licking for his pains. The idea of facing Dusty with a gun in his hand did not for an instant enter Willock's head.

Silence that could almost be felt had dropped on the camp, broken only by the thumping of Dusty's boots as he walked. Then old Boiler Benson spoke.

"Hosses coming, Cap'n Fog," he said, silently cursing the sound as it would most likely prevent Willock receiving a badly needed lesson in manners. "Not from the herd, along our back trail."

Immediately he heard the words, Dusty laid aside all his thoughts on Willock's redemption. With Goodnight still at the herd, it fell on the segundo to prepare for

meeting and dealing with unexpected, possibly un-
welcome visitors. So Dusty turned from the cowhand,
ready to rattle our orders.

For his part, Willock let out a sigh of relief. He decided
that he owed the approaching riders a vote of thanks, no
matter what brought them to the herd. In another five
seconds, he would have been forced to make a hateful
decision and either way he had gone would have been
unpleasant. So he listened to the approaching hooves and
mentally raised his hat.

> *"Come all you fellers, you cowhands from Texas,*
> *Bring on your young ladies and gather around,*
> *I'll tell you a story so sad and so gory,*
> *Of how Juan Ortega got put under ground.*
> *Ole Juan was a rowdy who never looked dowdy,*
> *He dressed caballero and died in his boots,*
> *Though his past was real shady, he loved but one lady,*
> *Her love caused the death of this king of owlhoots."*

Getting ready to leap to their *big* segundo's orders, the
trail hands settled down when a pleasant tenor voice lifted
over the sound of the hoofbeats. Clearly whoever came
did not intend to surprise the camp. Dusty relaxed before
the end of the first line, as did Red and Billy Jack, for they
had identified the singer's voice.

"It's Lon," Dusty told the oldtimer.

"That's the Ysabel Kid," Solly Sodak of the Lazy F
said, wanting to air his superior knowledge to the man at
his side. "He sure sings purty."

Satisfied that he had given notice of his coming, the
Kid did not continue with the "so sad and so gory" story
of Juan Ortega. Looking through the darkness, the men
by the fire soon made out enough to solve the matter of
the multiple hoofbeats. Though he was alone, the Kid had
four horses trailing about him with their hackamore reins
tied to his mount's saddlehorn.

Sitting afork his magnificent, huge white stallion—
which, despite its saddle and bridle, looked as wild as any
free-ranging mustang—the Kid rode into the light of the

flames before stopping. Swinging his right leg up and across the saddlehorn, he dropped lightly to the ground. In his right hand he gripped the new type of Henry rifle—soon to achieve fame as the Winchester Model of 1866, or the "old yellowboy" by virtue of its brass frame—given to him while helping Dusty in Mexico. An improvement on the original Henry, the rifle was much admired and several of the Swinging G's men swore they would save sufficient money from their end-of-trail pay to purchase similar weapons.

Travel-dirty, showing signs of having ridden far and hard, the Kid stood for a moment looking around the camp. From hat to boots, all his wearing apparel was black, including the gunbelt, which carried a walnut-handled Colt Dragoon revolver butt forward in the holster at the right side and an ivory handled James Black bowie knife sheathed at the left. Hair as black as the wing of a deep-South crow gave more hint of his Indian blood than did his red-hazel eyes and handsome, almost babyishly innocent cast of features. The eyes were alert, constantly watchful, almost alien in such a face. Dressed cowhand style, he gave the impression of latent, controlled, deadly danger, as a cougar did when sleeping on a limb.

"See you've got a fresh relay, Lon," Dusty greeted, knowing the four horses led by the Kid were not those he had taken to Mineral Wells.

"Left the others at the Swinging G and got some that weren't so tuckered out," the dark youngster explained. "Where-at's Colonel Charlie?"

"Out with the herd. He'll likely be back soon. Do you want to see him about something real important?"

"Sure. But it can wait until he gets back. I'll tend to my mount and eat. Then if he's not back, we'll ride out and meet him."

"I'll come and help you with 'em, Kid," Vern offered.

"Gracias," grinned the Kid. "We'll split it up fair. You tend to the relay and I'll see to ole Nigger here."

"I wouldn't have it any other way," Vern replied, walking across but waiting until the Kid released the horses and handed over the reins. Anybody who took liberties like approaching the white stallion too closely would right soon come to regret the indiscretion.

Talk welled up around the fire as the Kid and Vern departed toward the remuda with the horses. Looking around, Dusty noted gratefully that the tension had gone from the atmosphere. The Kid's arrival had given Willock a chance to let the show down against Dusty pass without losing face. So the cowhand resumed his seat during the conversation and stayed quiet, studiously avoiding making any movement or sound that might catch the small Texan's attention.

Not that Willock needed to worry about that. Satisfied that he had made his point, Dusty was quite prepared to let the matter drop. Later he might be compelled to prove himself by physical means, but felt content to wait until the moment was forced upon him. Dusty knew, as did the whole crew, that Willock had backed water. He would gain nothing and only increase any resentment Willock felt by emphasising the point. So, as far as Dusty was concerned, the incident had run its course and was at an end.

Helped by Vern, the Kid made good time in attending to the needs of his five horses. Leaving his stallion to roam free for the night, secure in the knowledge that it would come when needed, he turned the other four in with the remuda. Then, carrying his saddle, he returned to the fire. In passing, Vern exchanged scowls with Willock. However they both knew better than to resume their quarreling. They had come out of the first time without punishment, but Dusty would not deal so gently with them in the future.

The Kid had finished his meal and spread his blankets alongside Dusty's, then was about to suggest he and Dusty go out to meet Goodnight, when the rancher returned. Hearing his scout's request for an interview, Goodnight collected a meal and went to the bed wagon. With his plate on the tailgate, he stood with the Kid and Dusty in the light of the lantern which hung from the canopy's rear support. Interested eyes studied them from the fire, but none of the crew offered to come across and satisfy their curiosity.

"Looks like you've been moving, *Cuchilo*," Goodnight remarked, using the Kid's Comanche man-name "The Knife," granted with regard to his skill in using one.

"Some, *Chaqueta-Tigre*," The Kid answered, returning the compliment by addressing the rancher as "Jaguar Coat," given to him by his *Nemenuh** enemies in the days when he rode with Cureton's Rangers. "I trailed that feller clear up to Throckmorton, only he was traveling so fast I couldn't catch up to him, and I hadn't seen hide nor hair of Chisum neither. Got to thinking maybe the feller'd quit the Long Rail on account of them stolen cattle. Anyways, I was out of makings and with Throckmorton so close, I reckoned I'd ride in and buy some. I'm right pleased I did now."

"Apart from not believing the part about you *buying* tobacco," Dusty put in, "you're starting to get me interested."

"What I learned was——" the Kid began, speaking the deep-throated *Pehnane* dialect which Goodnight understood but Dusty did not.

"Talk U.S., you damned slit-eye," Dusty grinned. "I apologize, you did buy some tobacco—once."

"Cut the fooling, blast you!" Goodnight grunted, eyes sparkling good-humoredly. "You're worse'n two old women."

"I accepts that apology, sir," the Kid replied, bowing to the rancher. "Like I said, I'd got to thinking that feller'd quit Chisum and was getting all set to bawl Mark out for wasting my valuable time when I got back. Only it come out that ole Mark's smarter'n I figured—which he'd have to be comes to a point——"

"Is he always like this?" Goodnight groaned.

"You're seeing him at one of his better times," Dusty assured his uncle.

"Anyways," the Kid continued, after giving a lofty sniff. "Seems like Chisum'd been to Throckmorton, with

Nemenuh: "The People," Comanche Nation's name for themselves.

them Mineral Wells steers and left again—trail bossing a drive for some dudes who'd been around town for a spell."

"Did you see the dudes?"

"Nope, Colonel, they'd pulled out afore I got there."

"Where was Chisum driving to?" asked Dusty, although he could guess at the answer.

"Out to Fort Sumner. He'd left two days afore I got there, the dudes followed him later,"

"Damn it to hell, Dustine!" Goodnight barked. "You know what this means?"

"Yes, sir. Chisum's got near on a week's head start on us."

"It means a heap more than that. Chisum knows that trail as well as I do. He can stick to a route we'll have to follow and make sure that everything's spoiled after he's passed and afore we reach it. We'll never beat him to Sumner."

Dusty and the Kid exchanged glances which showed their complete agreement with Goodnight's coldly logical summation of the situation. With Chisum so far in the lead, they could not hope to push their herd fast enough to pass and beat him to their destination. Nor would Chisum hesitate to use foul means to slow them down. Unscrupulous he might be, but he was also a master cattleman and would know ways to effectively hinder a following trail drive. However, Dusty, the Kid and Goodnight sprang from stock which did not mildly admit defeat. So they gave thought to how they might still beat Chisum to Fort Sumner despite his advantages.

"I near on went after Chisum and gave him a mite of trouble collecting his herd after the stampede," the Kid remarked.

"Which stampede?" Dusty ejaculated.

"The one I was going to start," the Kid said calmly. "Only I figured you white folks'd likely not think I was playing fair. And that I'd best make speed to tell Colonel Charlie what I'd learned."

"Damned *Pehnane*," Dusty grunted. "You'd be better hunting buffalo with——"

"Hey though!" interrupted the Kid, coming as close as

the other two had ever seen to showing emotion. "If Chisum's using your trail, Colonel, he'll be going up the Clear Fork of the Brazos and across to the headwaters of the Pecos, won't he?"

"That's the trail Oliver Loving and I blazed," Goodnight admitted bitterly. "And, knowing Chisum, that's the way he'll go."

"Only you allus went up it earlier in the year," the Kid went on.

"We did!" Goodnight breathed, beginning to guess what the dark youngster was leading up to.

"And you never had any Injun trouble between the Clear Fork and the Pecos?"

"Not on that stretch."

"Only this's the time of the year when the *Kweharehnuh*'ll* be making their big buffalo and antelope hunting," the Kid went on. "If I know them, which I figure I do, they'll not take kind to having a damned great herd of cattle drove through their hunting grounds."

"That's for sure," Dusty agreed. "Which only makes things worse for us. Even if he manages to sneak his cattle through, Chisum'll make good and sure that the *Kweharehnuh*'re all riled up by the time we get there."

"So why go?" said the Kid.

"Because there's only one other way," Goodnight explained. "And it'd take us a damned sight longer to head south and circle around the Staked Plains. We'd still not get to Sumner on time."

The Kid's face was as gently innocent as a church pew full of well-behaved choirboys and his voice mild as he said, "I wasn't figuring on going 'round the Staked Plains."

Kweharehnuh: Antelope band of the Comanche Nation.

CHAPTER FIVE

Bad As It is It's Our Only Chance

For a long moment neither Dusty nor Goodnight spoke. Taken any way a man looked at it, the Kid had made a mighty startling—some would even say, considering his knowledge of the terrain involved—even crazy suggestion. The Staked Plains were a rolling, arid, semidesert area between the South Concho and Pecos Rivers. Baked by the heat, parched for the want of water, the stunted vegetation offered poor grazing and little shade for the cattle and many hazards existed along the route they would be forced to follow. Under no circumstances could it be termed the kind of country into which a trail boss would willingly direct his herd.

At last Goodnight let out a long breath and said, "It's near on ninety-six miles from the South Concho to the Pecos, Kid. With nothing but spike grass, horned toads and gila monsters from one side to the other."

"I knowed that all along," the Kid answered. "Back when I was a button with the *Pehnane*, I hunted desert sheep around it."

"We'll not be hunting around it, we'll be trailing cattle *across*," Goodnight pointed out. "There's not much drinking water, but plenty of alkali and salt lakes scattered about. Let a thirsty herd get just a teensy smell of one of 'em, and there'd be a stampede that nothing could stop. And any steer that drinks from one of them lakes'll be buzzard bait in twenty minutes."

"I know that, too," the Kid admitted.

For all his words, Goodnight was clearly giving the suggestion his close consideration. Watching his uncle, Dusty could almost follow the other's train of thought. Novel, wild, impractical though the Kid's idea might have sounded at first hearing, it was possibly their only chance of beating Chisum to Fort Sumner. The very nature of the animals in the herd made that so.

Unlike the pampered beef breeds which would follow them, the Texas longhorns lived in almost completely natural existence. Left to forage for themselves upon the unfenced ranges, they had over the generations developed the survival instincts of wild animals. In nature only the fittest survive. So any longhorn that reached maturity was perfectly capable of standing up to hardships and the rigors of climatic conditions.

Maybe, just maybe, the Kid had offered a solution to Goodnight's problem. Crossing the Staked Plains would be desperately risky, but better than no chance at all. No Texan ever cared to go down without fighting.

"Damn it!" Goodnight growled. "I'd hate like hell for Chisum and that slimy cuss Hayden to lick me this easy."

"And me," Dusty agreed. "Especially after they cost me the price of two new Stetsons."

"Two?" grinned the Kid. "Don't tell me that you lost that one you bought after them fellers shot up your old woolsey?"

"Somebody put a hole in the new one," Dusty explained ignoring the suggestion that he would wear a cheap, poor quality "woolsey" hat. "You haven't got kin around here, have you?"

"Damned if *I* don't start talking Comanche soon!" Goodnight groaned. "Kid, if you could find each of those lakes afore we come to it, we could point the cattle upwind until we get by and they won't smell the water."

"It'll not be easy doing, Uncle Charlie," Dusty cautioned.

"Don't I know it?" demanded the rancher grimly. "But, bad as it is, it's our only chance of licking Chisum to Fort Sumner."

"Which we all want to do, for more reasons than one. I tell you, Uncle Charlie, if we fail there'll be few who chance trying. And Chisum'll cheat 'em blind on taking their stock to sell for them."

"There's one thing in our favor," Goodnight said. "It's good grazing and easy going from here to the South Concho. So we'll let the steers take on fat and tallow up to there. After that, we'll push them day and night without stopping until we hit the Pecos. It'll be all of three-four days to get across."

"By then the crew'll've learned plenty about their work," Dusty replied and remembered something. "Hell's fire. We've got Dawn along. Maybe we should send her back."

"Whee doggie!" chuckled the Kid. "So that lil gal made it, did she? Way she talked 'n' acted going home, I got to figuring she had it in mind to come along. And I sure admire you, whichever of you's the one who's fixing to make her go back. That's no *Nemenuh naivi** as's been trained right 'n' proper from the cradle-board to do as the menfolks tells her regardless."

"What does delegation of authority mean, Dustine?" Goodnight inquired.

"'You do it, I'm scared to,' I've always been told. Poor ole Mark, I hope she don't chaw his ears off when *he* passes the word."

"Does she have to go back?" asked the Kid. "She's got sand to burn and spunk enough to see it through."

"Having her along might even help," Dusty went on. "No matter how tough the going, the fellers won't quit while she's sticking it out—and stick she will."

Naivi: unmarried Comanche girl.

"We'd best ask her how she feels about it, anyways," Goodnight decided. "And do it tonight, so's she's close enough to the Swinging G house to make it back without an escort; happen she wants to go."

"I'll bet my next month's pay that she's still with us at Fort Sumner," the Kid offered, looking at Dusty. "Are you on?"

"No bet. And anyways, you've already drawn most of your next month's pay to buy shells for that fool rifle."

"Injun-giver!"

"Are you figuring on telling the rest of the hands, Uncle Charlie?" Dusty asked, ignoring his friend's comment.

"What do you think?" asked Goodnight.

"I'd say no, was it me," Dusty decided. "At least until after they've been on the trail a mite longer."

Goodnight nodded soberly. Told of his intention of taking the herd across the Staked Plains, while still new to the notion of handling it, the Mineral Wells men might figure that they faced an imposssible task. After a few weeks on the trail, they would have widened their experience and, more important, gained at first hand complete confidence in the abilities of their trail boss and his segundo. Knowing they were led by competent, trail-wise bosses, the men would be more willing to risk the dangerous crossing.

"I think you're right," the rancher said approvingly. It seemed that his nephew had learned the lessons of leadership well; small wonder Dustine had done so well during the War and since. "When Dawn comes from the night herd, I'll tell her what we've decided and ask what she wants to do. Then I'll ask her not to tell any of the others."

"It'd be best," Dusty agreed.

On her return from riding the night herd, Dawn found herself taken to one side and told of Goodnight's intention to cross the Staked Plains. Without attempting to influence her one way or the other, he warned of the difficulties and dangers they would face. At the end, the girl stated her determination to see the drive through. Then she promised not to mention his plans, even to her brother. After a meal, she went to where her blankets were spread in the bedwagon. Allowing her to sleep there was the only concession the men made to her sex, but they agreed it was less embarrassing for all if she did not sleep among the male members of the crew.

Taking his horse—the big paint stallion which had crippled Ole Devil Hardin before Dusty tamed it for use as his personal mount*—from the picket line, the small Texan rode out to the herd. He had waited to see the girl's response to Goodnight's question, and left grinning a little at the calm manner in which she heard the startling news then gave her answer. As he drew near to the bedground, he could hear the droning, near-tuneless singing which experience had taught cowboys soothed the cattle and prevented them from becoming frightened by the unheralded appearance of a rider from the darkness.

> *"Now say, you fool critters, why don't you lay down?*
>   *And quit this for-ever moving around,*
>   *My hoss is leg-weary, my butt-end aches like hell,*
>   *So I could feel the bumps if I sat on a smell.*
>   *Lay down, you——bastards, lay down,*
>   *Lay down, you—— —— ——sons-of-bitches,*
>   *lay down."*

Looming from the blackness, riding at a leisurely walking pace, Swede Ahlén brought his song to a stop and grinned a greeting as he saw Dusty coming his way.

"That sure was a beautiful tune, Swede," complimented Dusty. "And the chorus would make a deacon proud."

"You should've heard the words Dawn was singing when we come out to relieve her," Ahlén answered, still grinning. "It like to start ole Billy Jack and me to blushing."

"I'll have to come out and listen next time she's on," Dusty decided. "Everything all right?"

"We've been quiet enough so far. Knowed we would

---

*Told in *The Fastest Gun in Texas*.

be, Billy Jack was saying how he figured we'd have a stampede come half an hour."

Turning in their saddles, the two men looked across the night-darkened range. Before them, the cattle were assembled in a loosely formed square with a rider patrolling each side. Experience and good luck had allowed the trail boss to pick a nearly perfect location, clear of ravines or draws into which a restless steer might blunder, or where wild animals could hide. Nor was there any wooded land, always a source of trouble and danger, close by. Some of the steers lay quietly chewing their cud, others slept on their feet. Here and there, a restless animal stirred a flurry of complaint as it moved from place to place in search of choicer grass on which to chew. However, having been pushed hard all day, allowed to feed on the way and carefully watered, the majority of the herd showed no inclination to travel.

Yet Dusty and Ahlén were aware of how easily the peaceful state could be changed. A sudden, loud, unexpected noise, the wind-carried scent of a passing predatory animal—be it cougar, wolf, black or grizzly bear—the appearance of a rattlesnake from a hole down which it had slipped during the day, any of them might send the cattle racing off in wild stampede. That was more likely to happen, however, when the steers were hungry, thirsty, riled up or disturbed for some reason; but the men knew better than to take unnecessary risks.

"Let's hope it stays that way," Dusty said after a moment's study of the herd. "Unless you feel like taking a gallop after them, that is."

"Happen I get to feel that way, I'll find me a tall tree and bang my head again' it to knock my brains back in," Ahlén grinned. Then he became sober and continued, "Say, Dusty. Burle Willock's got a big mouth, but he's a good hand."

"If he wasn't, I don't figure you'd've brought him along," Dusty replied.

"Yeah. Waal, I had me a lil talk with him afore I come out here and I don't reckon, what he said back, he'll give you any more lip or fuss."

"That's all I ask. I don't like billing in on things like that

tonight, but it had to be stopped. Young Vern
Sutherland's aiming to prove how he's a man grown on
the drive and I'd hate like hell to see him get pushed so
that he acted *loco* trying to do it."

"Burle was more'n a mite rough on him, and hadn't any
call to talk about having to carry him. Vern did all right
today. Damn it though, I've just now remembered——"

"What's up?" Dusty asked.

"Burle figures to be a real ladies' man," Ahlén
answered. "He got into some fuss with Darby Sutherland
over making up to Dawn the wrong way. Darby licked
him good and he's a bad forgetter."

"He'd better forget until this drive's over," Dusty
warned. "How d'you stand if I have to pick up his toes,
Swede?"

Ahlén knew what Dusty meant. Generally the term was
used to describe the punishment handed out to a remuda
horse which continually broke out of the wranglers' rope
corral, or a fractious steer making trouble in a herd.
Rather than have the difficult one stir up its companions,
or teach them its bad habits, the boss would order one of
his cowhands to pick up its toes. To do this, the man
roped the animal by its forefeet, bringing it crashing down
with sufficient force to knock some sense into it or break
its neck. In the latter case, the boss considered the loss of
the awkward one justified in that it preserved the
majority's good behavior.

While Dusty's intentions in Willock's case were
somewhat less drastic, his words conveyed the desired
meaning to Ahlén. If Willock did not mend his ways, the
small Texan intended to teach him a sharp and painful
lesson.

"Maybe we ride for the same brand back to home,
Dusty," Ahlén answered soberly. "But if it's to do with the
working of the herd and just between you 'n' him, he's on
his own. I know you won't play favorites when it comes to
picking up toes."

"You can count on it," Dusty assured him. "Well, I'll be
moving on to see if Billy Jack's fell off his hoss and broke
both his legs yet."

"Way he was talking coming up here, he's figuring on

that, or worse, happening any ole time," Ahlén replied. "Tell him to keep happy and cheerful."

"What do you want me to do?" Dusty asked. "Spoil his night."

For a moment Dusty wondered if he should tell Ahlén about the decision to cross the Staked Plains. Then he decided against doing so. Not that he distrusted the big man. Dusty knew Ahlén to be shrewd, capable, regarding him as one of the best hands in the crew and well worthy of the post of ranch foreman.

The latter was the deciding factor in not speaking. First quality of a ranch's foreman was the ability to put his own spread's interest foremost on all things. Being aware of the risks involved in making the crossing, Ahlén might feel it his duty to prevent his boss's stock being submitted to them. From what Dusty had seen, the other Mineral Wells men, with the possible exception of the D4S contingent, would follow Ahlén's lead. The big blond could either be a calming influence, or stir them up.

In the final analysis, the decision on whether to inform Ahlén or not lay with Goodnight. So Dusty concluded it would be best for him to go along with his uncle's original plan. With that in mind, Dusty left Ahlén to continue patroling and drifted on in search of Billy Jack.

"Howdy, Cap'n Dusty," the lanky cowhand greeted, halting his doleful and even more profane chorus of the night herders' chant as the small Texan came up. "Nice night, if it don't blow up a blue-norther or twister afore morning."

"Sure," Dusty agreed. "Everything going all right?"

"Up to now," Billy Jack answered, in a tone which expressed amazement that such should be the case. "Likely they'll all've died off by morning."

"Happen they have, Uncle Charlie'll likely peel your hide."

"Shucks! I knowed that I'd get blamed regardless. Did the Kid learn anything wherever he'd been?"

"A mite."

"Is that Wednesbury's partner still around, you reckon?"

"Not that I know of," Dusty replied. "He wouldn't get word about Wednesbury's try failing until it was too late to hit at us on the holding ground."

"He'll know by now," Billy Jack announced in gloomy satisfaction. "Likely got him a whole mess of hardcases coming after us by now."

"Could be," Dusty admitted. "Only Lon didn't see any of them on his way here and he watched real good."

Knowing Billy Jack, Dusty did not expect him to be comforted by the news. Letting out a long, tormented sigh, the lanky cowhand waved a languid hand at the resting cattle.

"This here herd'd spook real easy happen they come boiling up at us with guns a-roaring. Even if they ain't got any of that new-fangled diney-mite with 'em."

"Don't *you* let 'em do it," Dusty commanded.

"How'd I stop 'em?" Bill Jack wailed.

"Why, look to the heavens with the light of righteous truth, brother," Dusty suggested, sounding like a hell-fire-and-damnation circuit-riding preacher delivering a sermon, "and shout, 'They can't scare me, my soul is pure!' Then charge 'em head down and horns a-hooking."

"What if they figure I'm a stinking liar?" Billy Jack wanted to know, then he brightened up. "Anyways, they'd probably drop me in the first volley."

"We'll give you a swell burying," Dusty promised.

For all the light manner in which they discussed it, neither underestimated the danger. There had been at least two dudes involved in the bid to capture the Army's beef contracts, one of whom now lay in a grave at Graham's Boot Hill. Dusty did not expect Wednesbury's partner—or partners—to give up after the earlier setbacks, there was too much at stake for that. Those men were not interested in the welfare of Texas, but meant to carve a fortune out of the state's misfortune and poverty. There would be other tries at stopping Goodnight reaching Fort Sumner. So the trail crew needed to maintain a constant vigilance and be ready to counter force with force should the need arise.

At the moment Dusty gave his promise of a fine

funeral, a disturbance started close to where they sat. Coming on to a resting muley, one of the steers decided to drive it away out of sheer ornery cussedness. Instantly Billy Jack dropped his mournful pose and started his horse moving. Dusty waited until sure his help would not be needed, then rode on in search of the next member of the night guard.

Seeing the slim figure of Vern Sutherland approaching, Dusty brought his horse to a halt. There had been a slight stiffness in the youngster's attitude to him after the incident with Willock and he could guess at its cause. A faint grin twisted at the corner of Dusty's lips as he thought of the diverse nature of a segundo's work. It entailed far more than merely attending to the cattle, or ordering the trail hands to perform their tasks.

"Hi Vern," Dusty said.

"Cap'n!" Vern grunted and made as if to ride on.

"Hold it. Is something up?"

"Naw—Hell, yes there is. You didn't have to bawl down Burle Willock on my account. I could've took him."

"I didn't bawl him down on your account," Dusty corrected. "I made *both* of you quit doing something that somebody'd've been sorry for had it been done."

"I can handle a gun——!" Vern began hotly.

"So can most folks in Texas," Dusty interrupted. "Trouble being too many of 'em only learn *how* to shoot, not *when*."

"Burle Willock don't scare me!"

"And you don't scare him, so you're even," Dusty replied. "But, happen you pair make any more fuss on this drive, I'll make a stab at seeing if I can scare you both."

"Sure, Cap'n," Vern muttered, figuring that Dusty could make good his threat. "Only I don't cotton to having folks ride me."

"Ride you!" Dusty barked. "Did you hear the way they all rode Rowdy about his cooking?"

"Sure."

"Did he get riled?"

"No. He's only a cook——"

"You try doing without him. Or wait until you've got a

bust leg, or some other hurt," Dusty interrupted. "Then see how 'only' he is. Rowdy's as good a man as anybody on this drive. And because he is, and knows it, he takes a joke or more about his food. You're young, Vern, the youngest hand on the drive. So you'll get hoorawed some. But the fellers know that you're doing a man's work and figure you're grown enough to take a lil funning. Remember that next time somebody does it."

"Willock didn't mean it funny," Vern protested.

"Nor did you when you answered," Dusty pointed out. "Which I don't blame you for doing it. Sure, you've got to stand up and not be pushed around. All I ask is that you don't go to pushing back—afore somebody else starts."

"I'll mind it," Vern said.

"It'd be as well," Dusty replied. "See you around, Vern. Don't let Billy Jack give you the miseries."

Continuing his tour of the night guard, Dusty knew that he had caused Vern to think. He hoped that the youngster would take his advice and steer clear of further clashes with Willock. The drive would be difficult enough without adding a feud to its problems.

CHAPTER SIX
The Yap-Eaters're Tough Hombres

With only the barest touch of dawn's light showing, Rowdy Lincoln and his louse set to work rousing the trail hands. Already the coffeepots were steaming on the fire and the aroma of breakfast wafted to the groaning, cursing men the cook's racket tore from the arms of sleep.

Laying in his blankets, Vern listened to the comments hurled at Rowdy's head and began to see more than ever the point Dusty had made to him the previous night. So the youngster decided that he would avoid being touchy or easily riled in the future. If a mere cook could take joshing of a rough kind, a cowboy who was also a trail drive hand should be able to do just as well.

"Come on!" Dusty shouted, striding towards the bedwagon and banging his fist against the side. "It's near on noon and the crew're dying of sunstroke waiting to put their gear away."

"Looking for somebody?" Dawn inquired, walking from the far side of the wagon. "Us women folk're used to getting up early."

56

Collecting their food and coffee, the trail hands stood or squatted around the fire and began to eat. They ate without the formality of washing or shaving, stowing away the hot refreshments in the knowledge that they would receive no more until the herd had been bedded down that evening.

Having eaten, the hands dumped their plates and cups into the tub of hot water placed for that purpose. Then they rolled their blankets, secured the bundles holding their individual belongings and headed for the bedwagon. Each hand was responsible for seeing his, or her, bedroll went into the wagon. On the first failure to do so, the cook would attend to the matter and give the owner a tongue-lashing on their next meeting for his idleness. If the offender continued to leave his bedding unrolled, the cook was within his rights to drive off and leave it.

Already fed, the two day wranglers had collected the "cable" from the bedwagon. Taking the long, stout rope to where the night hawk held the remuda, the two men set up a temporary corral. Supporting the cable on forked sticks spiked into the ground, they formed it into an open U shape. Into that flimsy enclosure, the night hawk guided the horses.

Having been taught early the futility of fighting against a rope, the horses made no attempt to break through the slender barrier. So they milled around but remained inside the U while their users came to make the first selection of the day. With the trail hands, less the four on night guard, mounted and gone, the wranglers let the night horses join their companions. They did not start the remuda moving straight away, but waited for the night herders to return and change mounts.

Having relieved the night watch, the fourteen remaining trail hands took up their positions and watched for Goodnight's signal to start moving. Removing his hat, Goodnight swung it once counterclockwise over his head, then pointed it forward above the ears of his horse. Instantly Mark and Ahlén cut loose with a deep-throated, singsong chant which, they hoped, would eventually come to be regarded as marching orders by the steers.

"Ho, cattle!" boomed the two men. "Ho! Ho! Ho! Ho!"

Closing in, the trail hands began the business of getting the herd on the move. There was much the same kind of confusion as on the previous day, with an additional source of concern for the crew.

Even among the de-prided and impotent steers there was an inborn desire to lead. So, up toward the point, the largest or more aggressive of them started jockeying for position. It was a time of danger, calling for constant supervision by the swing and point riders, with powerfully muscled bodies thrusting and shoving in contests of domination.

Led by Dusty, Billy Jack, Red, Dawn and two more hands worked their horses in among the cattle ready to halt any serious conflicts. While most of the disputes, due to the press of advancing animals from behind, ended quickly, the work was not without risks. Separating two steers about to meet head-on, Dawn had her leg pinned between the saddle and the flank of a third longhorn. Saying a few things a well-bred young lady did not usually utter, the girl slashed at the steer with her rope and it drew away. Then she turned aside the rivals by the same means. Narrowly avoiding the stab of an angry steer's horns, Billy Jack's horse was butted by a muley and let fly with both hooves against the offender's jaw hard enough to make it allergic to butting for some time to come. In doing so, the horse nearly threw its rider. Recovering his balance with masterly skill, Billy Jack found fresh trouble. In passing, the steer stuck its horn up the left leg of his pants. The material tore before worse damage was done and the doleful cowhand spent the rest of the day moaning about his misfortune in having a new—well, not more than six months old—pair of levis torn to doll-rags.

Finally one steer, a ten-year-old heavyweight with a dark brown body and head and shoulders of black seemed to be asserting its dominance over all the others. Twirling like a flash, it met the challenges of potential rivals with such force and determination that all were scared off without fighting. At last it stalked off ahead of the rest and none questioned its right to do so. Falling in on either side of the self-appointed leader, Mark and Ahlén guided it in the required direction.

With the leadership determined, the cattle continued to move with increased ease and Dusty's party withdrew to the sides of the lines. Riding ahead, Dusty joined his uncle as Goodnight sat on a small rise to one side of the route.

"What do you reckon, Uncle Charlie?" Dusty inquired, nodding toward the point of the herd.

"I've seen that big cuss around. He always lived close to the house, so he's used to folk being around him. He's not mean, or snaky. Happen he can hold on to the lead, we'll be all right."

Like all herd-dwelling animals, the longhorns tended to follow the dominant male's directions. So a steady, well-behaved, sensible lead steer was invaluable on the trail drive. It would set the most suitable pace, obey the point riders' instructions without fuss and hold the rest of the cattle together by the strength of its presence.

Another day's hard pushing saw the trail herd thirty miles from the holding ground on the Swinging G. There was some horseplay around the campfire that night, but of a harmless nature. Dusty watched Willock to see how the cowhand was accepting the bawling out. From all appearances, Willock had decided to forget it, for he made no trouble and acted pleasantly enough in Dusty's presence. Yet he displayed a veiled hostility toward the entire D4S contingent, ignoring them completely. Nobody else seemed affected by Willock's attitude, so Dusty said nothing.

The events of the morning had prevented Dusty from suggesting to Goodnight that they should tell Ahlén of the change in their route. At nightfall, Dusty had put the matter from his mind and it was not raised.

The start of the third day's drive went off somewhat more smoothly and ended with the big brown and black steer even more firmly established as the leader. Due to its color, the trail crew started to call it "Buffalo" and it rapidly justified Goodnight's faith in it. It had all the qualities needed to lead the herd, being of a tractable nature where human beings were concerned and having the size, speed and bulk to handle dissidents or challengers, without being aggressive or bullying.

On the fourth day Goodnight allowed the pace to slacken. They were now well beyond the steers' regular stamping grounds, which caused a sharp reduction in the desire to return. Even the *ladinos* began to lose their eagerness to bolt, faced with unfamiliar surroundings, and took comfort from the companionship of the mass around them. While there was still the occasional attempt to break away, they grew infrequent and were easier to deal with. "Lone wolves" still prowled and circled the flanks of the herd, but the rest of the steers were gradually becoming accustomed to the trail.

By the end of the first week, the three thousand four hundred steers left—the early stages of a drive, with an inexperienced crew, always saw losses by desertion or from other causes—had settled into as near perfect a traveling unit as any trail boss could desire. Retaining its position as lead steer, Buffalo strode at the head of a long, multihued line of walking beef which stretched snake-like across the range. Following Buffalo came the chief contenders for his post of honor, the biggest, strongest, most energetic of the steers.

With each passing day, the order of seniority among the steers became more firmly established. Once on the move, they ambled along in the most convenient manner to their needs. Unless bunched together for some reason by the cowhands, they picked their own line of march as long as it was in the required direction and grazed as they walked. However, while a steer could drop back then revert to its original position, any attempt to advance beyond its station was resented and discouraged by the beasts ahead. So at any given time of the day a steer could generally be found in the same position relative to its companions. Even when thrown off the trail, stopped to allow more extensive feeding than possible on the march, or after being bedded down for the night, they would resume their positions on the drive's continuing.

The muley's soon formed themselves into a group for

mutual protection, bedding down clear of their horned kin, and foraged separately. Bringing up the rear, the weak, footsore or plain lazy animals formed a lachrymose bunch which needed to be constantly urged on by the drag riders.

Everybody on the drive worked hard from sunup until late in the afternoon. Even after that most of the hands faced a spell of riding the night herd. The cook and his louse might have things easy during most of the day, but made up for it by being the first of the crew awake every morning. Good at their work, they saw to it that the others were well-fed and kept the coffee on the boil all night for the benefit of the riders coming to or from the herd.

Not only the steers improved with the traveling. All the trail hands gained confidence and experience as the days went by. Dusty watched them all and drew his conclusions from what he saw. Although there was, naturally, some interranch rivalry, it stayed on a friendly basis.

Despite his start, Willock proved to be a good man at his work. He did tend to show off a mite and try to impress the others with his skill, but avoided incidents of the kind which had almost brought him into conflict with Dusty. Only once did his path close with Vern's; even then only slightly.

Apparently Vern had taken Dusty's comments of the first night to heart. He still reacted eagerly and showed boyish enthusiasm for his work, but not so much as on the first day of the drive. It seemed that Dawn too had profited from advice, for she might glance in annoyance when Vern acted in what she regarded as an unbecoming manner but never condemned him publicly. Left to himself, the youngster matured fast. He took part in the horseplay around the camp, giving as good as he got. When joshed about his youth, he no longer grew angry and commented instead on the age or senility of his tormentor. Only once did he almost fall from grace.

On the tenth day Goodnight allowed the herd to rest and graze. With Dusty's permission, Vern left camp on a hunting expedition in the hope of varying their diet. Shortly after noon he returned at a gallop on a lathered horse.

"I saw some dust shifting down that way, Cap'n," the youngster breathlessly announced, pointing along their back trail. "And there was something flashing in it."

"Best go take a look," Dusty decided and ordered some of the men to saddle up fast.

"Reckon it's that Hayden feller?" Vern asked excitedly, having been included in the party.

"I hope it's not," Dusty replied. "Let's ride."

Guided by Vern, the party rode east. On their way, they met the Ysabel Kid returning from a circle around the area. The Kid confirmed about the dust and explained the "metallic" flashes seen by Vern. About three miles away a large band of pronghorn antelope were grazing. What Vern had taken for the flickering of the sun on weapons was the flashing of the animal's white rumps as they signalled to each other in the manner of their kind.

Going back to the camp, the men told what had happened. Willock sneered about the mistake, but had sense enough to keep his comments to himself. All the older hands agreed that the youngster had done the right thing by returning. So their comments about his behavior held no sting. He redeemed himself by resuming his hunting in the late afternoon and returning with a bull elk, the meat of which made a welcome change from longhorn beef.

Having what appeared to be the easiest job on the drive, the Ysabel Kid came in for his fair share of ribbing whenever he appeared at the campfire. Ranging far ahead, or circling the herd at a distance, it was his duty to locate natural hazards, human enemies or any other kind of danger. He also had to report to the trail boss on the condition of the land ahead, so that the route offering the best, easiest travel could be selected.

With the possibility of further trouble from Hayden, the Kid kept an extra careful watch on the rear. Nor did Vern's abortive alarm cause the dark youngster to relax. However, day after day rolled by with no sign of their enemies. The weather stayed fine and the whole crew were in good spirits.

For all that he covered more miles than any of his companions in a given day, a convention had grown up in the camp to accuse the Kid of spending his time asleep in the shade of a bush and only catching up when sure all the work had been done. When the Kid tried to produce his leg-weary horses as vindication of his true hard-working qualities, Billy Jack countered by fabricating a story about a pretty girl the dark youngster visited each day.

Usually the Kid did not return until well after dark. So Dusty and Goodnight, out ahead of the herd, regarded his appearance with apprehension when he came toward them in the late afternoon of the fourteenth day. Nothing showed on the Indian-dark young face and its owner might have been no more than returning in the normal course of events. Yet Dusty and the rancher guessed that the kid bore grave and disturbing news.

"All right," Dusty said resignedly as his *amigo* halted the leggy *bayo-lobo** horse he was using that day. "What's up ahead."

"Plenty of good grass, a stream of clear water and a mighty pretty place to bed down just by it."

"Now the bad news," Goodnight ordered.

"Saw some smoke ahead a ways," the Kid complied.

"Indians making it?"

"Could be, Colonel. It was a fair ways off and I didn't take time to go closer. Figured you'd want to know."

"You figured right. What do you reckon?"

"There wasn't enough smoke for white folks to be making it. Or for a whole village. I'd say it's a small bunch. Out raiding seeing's how they're down this ways."

Which meant, as Dusty and Goodnight knew, the braves were on a horse-stealing mission. Not a comforting thought when the herd had along almost seventy good horses in its remuda. During his time with Cureton, Goodnight had gained a considerable knowledge of the Comanche as enemies. However, he was willing to yield to

---

Bayo-lobo: dun approaching wolf grey color.

the Kid's superior wisdom.

"What're our chances, Lon?"

"I dunno," the Kid answered frankly. "Down here's the borders of the *Kweharehnuh* and *Yamparikuh* stamping grounds. Could be a bunch from either. I'd bet my money on it being Yap-Eaters, not Antelopes, at this time of the year."

"The Yap-Eaters're tough *hombres*," Goodnight pointed out.

"Sure, but us *Pehnane* were allus closer to 'em than to the Antelopes. Happen it's either band and not just a bunch of *tuivitsi* on their lonesome, I might be able to get us by them. It'll likely cost us some cattle, and maybe a few of them extra hosses I asked you to fetch along."

"It'll be worth them to get by without fuss," Goodnight stated. "Only a bunch of hot-headed young bucks aren't likely to listen to reason."

"Nope," agreed the Kid. "But, happen them *tuivitsi*'ve got a *tehnap* along, he might be."

"Can you get up close enough to talk, even if there is one along? "Goodnight asked, knowing that even *tehnap*, experienced warriors, were inclined to shoot first and ask questions a long ways second when dealing with white men.

"I've got my medicine boot along," the Kid answered. "When they see that, they'll sit back and listen."

"You want to handle it alone?" asked Dusty.

"Nope. I'd like to have you along to talk for Colonel Charlie. There's another thing, you mind how them renegade Tejases took on when they saw what our new Henrys could do?"

"I sure do," Dusty grinned, recalling how the repeated fire from their Winchesters had scared off a band of Indians while on a mustang-catching trip.* "It's likely those Yap-Eaters won't have seen rifles like them yet either."

"Go with him, Dustine," Goodnight said, even though he might be sending his favorite nephew to an unpleasant

---

*Told in *.44 Caliber Man*.

death. "Make any kind of deal you have to and I'll back you on it."

"Yo! When do you want to start, Lon?"

"As soon as we've fed, I'd say. Further we are from the herd when we meet 'em, the easier we can dicker."

Accompanied by Dusty and the Kid, Rowdy speeded up his team and made for the site selected as their night's camp ground. There he and his louse broke all records in producing a meal. So well did they work that Dusty and the Kid rode out of camp just as the first of the night watch came from the herd.

"Back to four of us on night herd," Willock muttered sullenly, watching the Kid and Dusty pass by. "There's something in the air!"

"What's up, Rowdy?" inquired Raymar of the Flying H, having seen the decorative buckskin case across the Kid's bent left arm. "What's Lon got that medicine boot on his rifle for?"

"Had he?" countered the cook and raised his eyes piously to the sky. "So help me, I never noticed."

"There's something bad wrong!" Willock insisted.

"That stew don't smell no worse'n any other night," Spat Bodley objected. "And if it's anything else, we'll likely get told soon enough."

However the four men had to return to their duties with curiosity unsatisfied. Goodnight gave them no more than the usual orders before following the rest of the crew to the camp. There he addressed the party at the fire and warned them what the Kid suspected.

"Comanches!" Dawn breathed.

"Shucks, they don't fight at night, sis," Vern protested. "Everybody knows that."

"They may not fight, but they move and raid in it," Goodnight warned him. "Only, afore you start looking for war-whoops behind every rock, I don't reckon they're close enough to make fuss for us tonight. Sure, I know I doubled the guard. I'd sooner have you all out riding the night herd and see nothing than get two men jumped and the cattle scattered.

"Uncle Charlie's got a real kind heart," Red whispered

to Dawn. "You've just to look real hard to find it. Most of my uncles're like that."

Despite his comment, Red fully agreed with Goodnight's precautions. So did the rest of the listeners. Throwing a glare at his nephew, the keen-eared rancher continued with his orders in case of an attack.

"What repeating rifles have we along?" Goodnight asked, wanting to make sure he knew the correct figure.

"All my boys're carrying Spencers, down to Rowdy and Turkey——"

"*Up* to Rowdy 'n' Turkey," corrected the cook, a privileged member of rangeland society. "That's the right way to say it."

"I've a new Henry," Mark announced.

"Pappy let me bring along our Henry," Vern went on, not without a touch of pride. "But Dawn's only got her old scattergun."

"It's a right handy tool though," Dawn continued tolerantly.

Altogether the party could muster twelve repeating rifles and carbines, the rest of the crew being armed with muzzle-loaders, single-shot breech-loaders or just their handguns. Quickly Goodnight arranged the positions of the trail crew so that the repeaters would be evenly shared between the swing, flank and drag. Should the Indians come looking for trouble, the flank and swing riders on each side were to join their respective point man at the head of the herd. The drag hands and wranglers had orders to gather at the wagons. That way there would be controlled groups of defenders delivering volley firing instead of scattered individuals shooting.

"Hey, Colonel Charlie!" Rowdy Lincoln suddenly hissed. "There's somebody moving out there to the east."

CHAPTER SEVEN

This Is Why You Won't Take Our Cattle

Having wanted mounts which they could trust and rely upon under any conditions, Dusty had collected his big paint stallion from the remuda while the Kid whistled up his magnificent white. From his war-bag in the bedwagon, the Kid had produced a long, heavily fringed buckskin pouch decorated with medicine symbols. With that on his rifle, it told all who knew the *Pehnane* that he belonged to the Dog Soldier lodge. So any insult or injury inflicted upon him would bring reprisals from the rest of that savagely efficient fighting brotherhood.

With a good meal inside them and a reserve of pemmican in case of emergency, the two *amigos* wasted no time in heading across the range. Two miles beyond the herd, the Kid brought his horse to a halt as he wished to take certain added precautions before visiting the Comanche camp.

In addition to gathering the medicine boot from his gear, the Kid had donned a pair of *Pehnane* moccasins. Clearly he did not intend relying on such a flimsy disguise.

Dismounting, he handed Dusty the buckskin-encased Winchester, removed his gunbelt and hung it across the white's saddle. Then he stripped off his hat, shirt, bandana and levis. That left him clad only in the moccasins and a breechclout of traditional *Nemenuh* blue. Formed of a length of cloth drawn up between the legs and passed under a belt at front and rear, with loose-hanging flaps trailing almost to knee level, the garment served him instead of conventional white man's underclothing and allowed a rapid transition to an Indian warrior when necessary.

Stripped of his cowhand regalia, the Kid looked almost completely Indian. Nor did the gunbelt lessen the likeness after he buckled it on. Many a brave-heart warrior wore such a rig, looted in battle. Satisfied with his appearance, he made a bundle of his clothes and fastened them to the saddle's cantle. Catching the rifle Dusty tossed to him, he vaulted astride the white's seventeen-hand high back.

"Let's go," the Kid suggested. "This way, happen any of 'em see us, they'll be more likely to talk first."

Holding their horses to a fast, mile-devouring trot, they rode to the west. Night came, but the Kid had seen enough of the suspicious smoke to have fixed its position firmly. Despite the darkness, he led the way in as near a direct line as possible. After about three hours' riding, he signaled Dusty to stop.

"It's not far ahead now, so you'd best stay put until I've been in and let 'em know how things stand."

"Go to it," Dusty replied. "Only if they're all *tuivitsi*, you come back here *pronto*."

"You can count on it," the Kid assured him.

"What do you want me to do?"

"Wait here. I'll move in on foot. Watch ole Nigger and come up with him when he starts moving. He'll soon enough let you know if there's anybody sneaking around. Should there be, try to settle 'em without too much noise."

"Is it all right if I whomp 'em on the head with my carbine?" Dusty inquired, sliding the Winchester from its saddleboot.

"'S long's you do it polite and thank 'em for letting you," replied the Kid.

With that the dark youngster dropped from his horse's back. He landed and disappeared into the blackness with the minimum of sound. Cradling the carbine on his left arm, Dusty remained astride the big paint. At his side the white stallion stood like a statue, only its raised head, pricked ears and constantly moving nostrils testifying to its alertness as it sought for any warning scent or sound.

Advancing on noiseless feet, the Kid looked no less wild and vigilant than his horse. He came across no guards, nor expected to find any despite the increasing evidence which reached his ears of the Indians' presence in the vicinity. Almost half a mile from where he had left Dusty, he received his first sight of their quarry. Reaching the lip of a draw, he looked down its gentle slope at the fire which had sent up the smoke that brought him from the herd.

A touch of relief crept over the Kid at what he saw, along with a feeling of satisfaction at having his judgment verified. There were only men around the fire on the bottom of the draw. Not more than thirty of them, stocky, medium-sized and wearing clothes made from buckskin, elk hide, but not antelope. Naturally the bulk of the party consisted of *tuivitsi*, young, comparatively inexperienced warriors. Yet the Kid could see sufficient *tehnap* and a warbonnet chief present to ensure that his medicine pouch would be respected and himself allowed to speak unmolested. They were a well-armed band, if a touch low on firearms and with no repeating rifles. By their dress, they came from the *Yamparikuh* band, not the *Kweharehnuh*.

Continuing just as quietly down the slope, the Kid halted while still in the darkness. So far none of the party gave any sign of being aware of his presence, but he wanted to announce himself before appearing.

"Greetings, men of the *Yamparikuh*," the Kid called, speaking the *Pehnane* dialect perfectly. "I come in peace to your fire."

At the first words, several of the *tuivitsi* sprang to their feet and reached for weapons. None of the *tehnap* moved and the chief showed no sign of agitation, accepting that only a member of the *Nemenuh* could come so close undetected.

"You may come," the chief replied.

Given permission, the Kid walked into the fire's light. He heard several startled comments as the men saw his tall, slim, un-Comanche figure coming out of the night. However the *Nemenuh* had adopted enough captive children into the tribe, turning the boys into warriors every bit of "The People" as if they had been Comanche-born, for the Yap-Eaters to accept his *bonafides*. And that *was* a Dog Soldier's medicine pouch covering the vistor's rifle. Halting before the chief, the Kid raised his right hand in the peace greeting.

"I am one called *Pinedapoi*," the chief introduced. "Are you *Nemenuh*?"

"My grandfather is Long Walker of the *Pehnane*," the Kid answered. "I am one called *Cuchilo*."

"You speak an honored name. Long Walker is a respected chief of our people. And I have heard of *Cuchilo*."

"The fame of *Pinedapoi* has reached my ears," the Kid countered politely.

"It is said you are a white man now," a leathery *tehnap* put in.

"I have friends among the white men and live in their lodges," the Kid admitted. "But I am still *Nemenuh*." He paused to see if there would be a challenge to his statement. None came and he went on, "My blood brother waits in the darkness, wishing to speak with the chief and braves of the *Yamparikuh*. He is a name-warrior among his people. His name is Magic Hands."

"The man who broke the medicine of the Devil Gun?" asked *Pinedapoi*.

"He is the one," confirmed the Kid.

During the War, a pair of fanatical supporters of the Union had obtained an Agar Coffee Mill gun and hoped to use its rapid-fire qualities to lead the Indians in Texas on the warpath. Dusty had learned of the plot, attended the council at which the gun was to be displayed, killed the fanatics and prevented the full-scale uprising they had planned.*

"He may come," *Pinedapoi* declared, for such a fighter as "Magic Hands" would be welcome even though a white man and nominally an enemy, and without the added advantage of being blood brother to a member of the *Phenane* Dog Soldiers.

The Kid pursed his lips and gave a shrill whistle. In the darkness, Dusty saw the white stallion toss its head and start to walk forward for no reason apparent to him. Following the horse, he booted his carbine. Riding toward the Yap-Eaters' camp, Dusty felt a touch uneasy. Cold black eyes in impassive slightly Mongoloid faces studied him from head to toe. At a signal from the Kid, the stallion halted on the fringe of the firelight. Taking his cue from Nigger, Dusty stopped his paint, dropped from the saddle and let the reins dangle free. With his horse ground-hitched, he walked to where the Kid and the chief waited.

"Why are you here, Magic Hands?" *Pinedapoi* asked in Spanish after the formalities had ended.

"I am with *Chaqueta-Tigre*," Dusty explained in the same language. "We are taking a herd of cattle to the Army's forts beyond the Staked Plains."

"So that the soldiers may eat well and be strong to fight against the Comanche?" suggested the chief. "Or to make your home on the Indian lands?"

"Neither. To feed the Indians who live at peace on the reservations."

Before Dusty could elaborate further, a *tuivitsi* rose and pointed to the south. All the other young braves came to their feet, talking and showing excitement. The older warriors scowled their disapproval at such behavior before strangers and retained their impassive postures.

*Told in *The Devil Gun*.

"We've got callers, Dusty," the Kid said quietly. "A wagon and two-three riders. Could be we've picked a might poor time to come calling."

"Could be," Dusty agreed. "Only it's too late to pull out now."

In a short time the newcomers appeared and Dusty found that the Kid had guessed correctly about the composition of the party. Three riders flanked a small wagon and two men sat on its box. They were Mexicans, evil-faced and looking out of place in the tarnished finery of their *charro* clothing. All carried revolvers and knives at their belts, while one of the riders nursed a Spencer carbine on his knees.

"Damn the luck!" grunted the Kid. "It's Hugo Salverinas and his bunch. They're *Comancheros*. That's Salverinas on the wagon. The driver's Andrés. The short cuss riding on the right's Carlos, the one with the Spencer's called León and the other's Cristóbal. If the Devil put worse on this earth, I've sure never met 'em."

Which, considering some of the people met by the Kid during his short but hectic life, sounded very damning for the new arrivals. *Comancheros* were Mexican *bandidos* who combined trading with the *Nemenuh* and raiding on their own account. Merciless killers, they had been all but quelled by the Texas Rangers before the War and returned due to the inefficient policing offered by the corrupt Davis Administration currently controlling the state.

Dusty could not see a bunch of *Comancheros* taking kindly to finding two Texans in the Comanche camp. Nor could the Kid, so he moved slowly from his companion's side and squatted on his heels by the fire. The wagon came to a halt and Salverinas directed a cold glare in Dusty's direction. Short, heavy-built, cruel-featured, the man carried himself with the air of one who knew he was on safe ground.

"Who is this?" Salverinas demanded, pointing at the small Texan but apparently taking the Kid for one of the *Yamparikuh*.

"He is a friend," *Pinedapoi* answered, sounding just a

touch annoyed at the tone of the *Comancheros'* leader.

"Why is he here?" Salverinas went on without leaving the wagon's box.

"Why are *you* here?" countered the chief.

"We met Apache Scalp and four braves," Salverinas explained in a milder voice and his men swung from their horses. "They told us where you are camped and we came to bring you news. Not far from here is a large herd of cattle. If you take them for us, we have guns, powder and lead for trading."

"What do you say to this, Magic Hands?" *Pinedapoi* asked, the conversation having taken place in Spanish.

"He is sending many of your braves to the Land of Good Hunting, chief," Dusty replied. "We want no trouble with your people. And you have too few braves to attack *Chaqueta-Tigre's* herd with any hope of winning."

"They are not more than twenty-five men," Salverinas put in. "You have thirty here and more around if you need them."

"We are all well armed," Dusty warned. "Not only with handguns. We have many rifles."

"The *Yamparikuh* have faced rifles before——" Salverinas began, as Dusty hoped he would.

"But not such rifles as our men carry," the small Texan stated, dipping his left hand into a pocket and producing something which he handed to the chief. "This is why you won't take our cattle."

"What is it?" *Pinedapoi* inquired, turning the metal-case Henry cartridge between his thumb and forefinger.

"A bullet such as our new rifles fire. Each of them can be loaded and fired many times without reloading——"

"We have such a rifle here!" Salverinas barked. "It holds seven bullets and they cannot be loaded quickly."

"Our rifles are of a new, better kind," Dusty told him. "And it will not be *you* who face them."

Squatting on his heels to one side of his companion, the Kid grinned and slid the medicine boot from his rifle. Trust old Dusty to say just the right things. *Pinedapoi* and the *tehnap* particularly could see how the metal-case bullets might speed up the reloading process, even beyond that of paper cartridges which required that the weapon be capped separately. While a Comanche had few peers for courage, once he passed the *tuivitsi* stage he also knew the value of caution. Using single-shot rifles and the new bullets, a respectable rate of fire could be achieved. High enough to make attacking men armed with such weapons a costly business.

Equally aware of the Comanches' qualities, Salverinas read the signs as well as had the Kid. The *Yamparikuh* would hesitate to throw their lives away, but he saw another way by which he might achieve his ends.

"This small *Tejano* must be very important if he comes and speaks for the men with the cattle," Salverinas said, jumping from the wagon. "Take him prisoner and his friends will pay well to have him returned."

"I can't do that," *Pinedapoi* objected. "Magic Hands is my guest."

"But not mine!" Salverinas spat out. "If I take him——"

"That is between you and him," the chief answered calmly.

"Get him!" the *Comanchero* ordered and the three men left their horses to move in Dusty's direction.

Instantly the Kid rose, landing lightly on spread-apart legs. He held the Winchester in his right hand, thumb over the wrist of the butt, forefinger inside the triggerguard and the remaining three fingers curled through the loading lever's ring, its barrel directed at the ground. Mutters rose from the watching *Yamparikuh* as they realized that he held some new kind of rifle.

For their part, the three Mexicans studied the new element which had entered the game. At that moment the Kid did not look white. The fire's light played on his all but naked, hard-muscled and wiry body, its torso marked with the scars of old wounds. Standing before them, he looked like some great cat ready to pounce, or a Comanche Dog Soldier on the prod.

"*Pinedapoi* said for your boss to take him, *pelados*!" growled the Kid.

Although the words came in English, with the

exception of the final insulting name—used in that manner it meant a corpse or grave robber—the trio understood. More than that, they knew no Comanche was addressing them. Sure he looked and acted like the saltiest brave who ever put on the paint and rode the war trail, but he spoke Texan like one of the Alamo's defenders. To men from the Rio Grande's bloody border country, the combination brought a name to mind.

"Cabrito!" ejaculated León, conscious of his Spencer's comforting weight and the fact that he held it in a better position of readiness than did the dark young Texan.

"That's me," agreed the Kid. "Now, happen you want to take a hand, get to it."

Quickly Salverinas assessed the situation and knew that, *Cabrito* or not, he must act. The Comanches had no respect for a coward or a boaster. Should he fail to back up his suggestion, he would be lucky to leave the camp alive. Taken any way he looked, things seemed to be in his favor. Not only was he fast with a gun, but his driver had already slid the short-barreled shotgun from its boot on the side of the wagon box. That small *Tejano* wore two guns, yet hardly seemed dangerous. Which left the Ysabel Kid. *Cabrito* was good, Salverinas did not deny that. So were the three men facing him. It was worth a chance. With the two Texans dead, the *Yamparikuh* would attack and scatter the herd. That ought to provide pickings for the *Comancheros*; not the least being the opportunity to obtain some of the repeating rifles.

"Get them!" Salverinas ordered, stabbing his right hand fast toward the ornate butt of his holstered Colt.

That left the others with no alternative but to fight. *Cabrito* would not waste time in asking what their intentions in the matter might be. So León started to swing his Spencer into line, confident that he was in a better position than the Kid to aim and fire. To the right of the trio Carlos reached for the fighting knife sheathed at his belt. On the left, Cristóbal put his trust in the power of his Army Colt.

Working with lightning fast precision, the Kid selected the men in order of their threat to his life. From his findings, he made his plan of campaign and put it into effect. First to go, without any argument, must be León for he already held a weapon in his hands.

Up swung the Winchester's barrel, its foregrip slapping into the Kid's left palm as if drawn there by a magnet, to line unerringly on the man with the Spencer. Flame lashed from the muzzle and a flat-nosed B. Tyler Henry-designed bullet tore its way into León's chest before he could complete turning his Spencer toward its mark. Wanting to impress the *Yamparikuh* with the magazine capacity and rapid-fire potential of the Winchester, the Kid fanned the lever through its loading cycle. In trained hands, the rifle could throw out two bullets per second; and the Kid possessed the necessary skill to achieve that performance. Working the barrel across the deal with the next danger, he got off four shots which all found their way into the reeling Mexican's body. Thrown backwards, León died without managing to line his Spencer or get off a load in return.

Blurring down the lever, the Kid watched an empty cartridge case flick out of the ejection slot in the top of the frame. Automatically counting his shots, he swung the barrel at the second most dangerous of the trio. Cristóbal might be trying to draw his revolver, but the Kid new Carlos would beat him into action. Out came the knife, with Carlos drawing it rearward for a deadly underhand throw. Only a bullet, propelled by twenty-eight grains of prime du Pont powder, flew faster than even the best-designed knife. Again the Winchester spat and Carlos jolted under the impact of lead. Already the knife was flying in the Kid's direction. On firing, he flung himself aside. While moving, he continued to shoot. Steel nicked his arm, so close did it come, but he had carried himself clear of the worst effect. Another bullet struck Carlos, turning him around and tumbling him on to his face.

Cristóbal had his revolver drawn, but he hesitated before trying to use it against a fast-moving target. Bringing it up, he aimed from shoulder high on where he

figured the Kid would land. As he fell, the Kid stopped
shooting. Aware that he could not use the rifle from waist
level while on the ground, he thrust it forward. Seeing the
Kid land, Cristóbal made a hurried last moment of
adjustment of his aim and fired. To miss. As soon as his
body touched the ground, the Kid rolled over and the
bullet ploughed into the dirt where he had been an instant
before. Settling on his belly again, he cradled the butt of
the Winchester against his shoulder. A cold red-hazel eye
peered from the rear sight to the blade at the muzzle end
of the barrel. When both were set to his satisfaction,
which took a bare half second, his forefinger gently
squeezed the trigger. Striking Cristóbal in the head, the
bullet from the rifle instantly ended further attempts on
the Kid.

Ignoring the blast of shooting sparked off by the Kid,
Dusty sent his hands flashing across. Fingers closed on
the white handles of the waiting Colts and a thumb coiled
around the spur of each's hammer. Almost faster than the
eye could follow, the long-barreled Army Colts left
Dusty's holsters. Only one of them roared. From waist
high, in what would soon become known as the
gunfighter's crouch, Dusty fired his left-hand revolver.

Shock twisted at Salverinas' face as he realized that the
insignificant cowhand so lightly dismissed was a *big*,
lightning-fast, dangerous man. Then a .44 ball spiked a
hole between the Mexican's eyes. He turned involuntar-
ily, the gun still not clear of his holster, and tumbled to the
ground.

Slower than the others to access the danger, the driver
completed the freeing of the shotgun and started to throw
it to his shoulder. Salverinas had advanced from the
wagon which permitted Dusty to deal with him from the
gunfighter's crouch. Not wanting to chance shooting by
instinctive alignment over the distance separating him
from the other Mexican, Dusty took the time to swing his
right hand Colt to shoulder level. The wisdom showed as
the gun spat. Caught in the chest by its load, the man tilted
backward. With a roar the shotgun sent the charges from

its barrels harmlessly into the air. Then he fell into the wagon, his feet sticking into the air, twitching for a few seconds and going still.

Two *tuivitsi* sprang to the heads of the wagon's team, preventing them from bolting. After a glance to make sure that Salverinas was out of the game, Dusty turned to look at the Kid.

"Did they get you, Lon?"

"Just a nick," the dark youngster replied, coming to his feet. "Throw me some more bullets and we'll start to dicker with *Pinedapoi*."

CHAPTER EIGHT

You are Responsible for Our Deaths

Listening in the silence which followed the cook's warning, the girl and men about the trail camp's fire detected faint sounds to the east. Then they awaited Goodnight's orders, being all too aware that none of the crew, or other friends that they knew of, should be moving about in that direction. There might be a simple, or harmless explanation for the sound, but the bearded rancher did not aim to risk it being so.

"Grab your rifles!" Goodnight barked. "Drag and right side men stay by the wagons. Wranglers head for the remuda. Rest of you, out to the herd if anything busts. Move it!"

Swiftly the party scattered. So that all might gain experience in every aspect of trail driving, the crew had been alternating their positions from point to swing, flank or drag. Yet there was no confusion, each member snatching up a firearm and heading to the appropriate group. Holding her shotgun, Dawn slid under the bedwagon and rested its twin-tubes on a spoke of the rear wheel. A moment later Billy Jack, carrying a Henry "liberated" on the battlefield during the days when he had ridden as Dusty's sergeant major, dropped to her left side. Showing excitement and a touch of eager anticipation, Vern joined them. Red Blaze, armed with a Spencer obtained from the same source which had supplied Billy Jack's Henry, stood by the tailgate. The remainder of the wagons' defenders had also selected places from which they could fight in reasonable safety.

"Likely we'll all be killed 'n' scalped comes morning," Billy Jack muttered to the girl.

"How'd I get you for a partner?" Dawn whispered back.

"Just fortunate, I reckon," the lanky one answered. "Being with me, you're sure to get killed early."

By which time the suspicious noises in the night had come closer and were identifiable. Listening to the rumble of wheels mingled with the beating of hooves, Vern let forth a snort of disappointment.

"A wagon and hosses!" the youngster announced. "I never heard tell of Injuns riding the war trail in a wagon."

"There's always a first time for everything," Red told him.

"Hello the fire!" called a voice from the darkness. "Can we come in?"

"It's white folks!" Vern sniffed and began to wriggle forward.

"Stay put until Colonel Charlie tells you different!" ordered Billy Jack in a low, grim tone far removed from his normal plaintive whine. In that moment he let Dawn and Vern see him as he really was, a bone-tough competent fighting man. Such a change did it make that Vern froze as if turned to stone.

"Come ahead," offered Goodnight. "But do it slow, easy and with your hands showing."

Time dragged by, with the trail crew remaining at their posts. While the second group had joined their night horses, Mark had not led them out to the herd. He was waiting to make sure that doing so would be necessary. From what he had just heard, the need ought not to arise;

but he kept the men by their mounts until certain of it.

Drawn by a pair of powerful horses, a small covered wagon came into the light of the fire and stopped. It was driven by a medium-sized, dapper, handsome man, with an exceptionally beautiful, black-haired young woman seated at his side. From all appearances, neither of them belonged to the range country. The man wore a well-cut town suit which set off his slender frame to its best advantage, derby hat, spats and walking boots—as opposed to the high-heeled cowhand variety. A wide brimmed, flower-decorated hat graced the woman's head. Draped across her shoulders, a black cloak hung open at the front. Under it she wore a stylish black dress with a décolletage which seemed more suited to a fancy dude ball than for riding in a wagon on the West Texas plains. Jewelry sparkled at her ears, neck, wrists and fingers, while the dress displayed a truly magnificent figure.

A second man rode alongside the wagon. No dude this, but a product of the West. Tall, well-made, clad in range clothes and with a low-hanging Army Colt at his right thigh, his surly features and general attitude told a story to eyes which could read the signs. A cattle-town loafer, a hired hardcase, but no cowhand. Not the kind of man one would expect to find with such elegant traveling companions.

For all his surprise at the sight, Goodnight retained his poise and remembered the social conventions.

"Get down and rest your horses, ma'am, gents," he said. "Food's on the fire and you're welcome to spend the night here."

"My thanks, sir," the driver replied, swinging deftly to the ground and walking forward. "My name is Edmond de Martin and the lady is my sister, Barbe."

"My pleasure, ma'am," Goodnight said, formally removing his hat and bowing to the girl. He was conscious that the men had come from their places of concealment, or returned from the picket line, and stood staring with undisguised interest at the wagon, or rather at its occupant.

"Good evening," Barbe greeted. Like her brother, she

spoke with a slight foreign accent. "Would somebody please help me down?"

Watching with a mixture of amusement and disapproval, Dawn could not remember when Vern had moved with such alacrity. Nor were the majority of the men any slower in offering their services. Soon most of the crew milled around the wagon like cattle attracted by the blood call, pushing, shoving and trampling on each other's feet in their eagerness. Letting out a sniff, Dawn stalked over to the crush.

"Back off afore you turn the son-of-a-bitching wagon over!" she snapped. "Come on. You can't all lay hold and lift her down."

Barbe flashed a surprised glance at the speaker and lost her smile for a moment. Hostility mingled with the surprise on the newcomer's face before it regained its original expression.

"The young—er—lady is right, gentlemen," Barbe said, causing a hurried withdrawal of the closest men. "If one of you will help me——?"

"Thin out there, some of you!" Goodnight ordered. "See to Miss de Martin, Dawn, Swede. Mark, take out pickets for the night."

"Yo!" Mark replied. "Come on, move it some of you."

"Are you expecting trouble, Colonel Goodnight?" asked de Martin, watching the men scatter. His sister descended from the wagon with the minimum of aid from Dawn. "I assume that you are Colonel Charles Goodnight?"

"I am, sir. My apologies for not introducing myself sooner."

"I judge by how you acted as we approached that you are expecting trouble."

"There may be Comanches about," Goodnight admitted. "Don't alarm your sister. I doubt if we're in any immediate danger, but I'd sooner not take chances."

"That's wise," de Martin agreed. "And if there are Indians about, I am doubly fortunate in finding you tonight. With Mr. Heenan for our guide, my sister and I have been following you for the past ten days or so."

"May I ask why?"

"To accompany you to Fort Sumner."

"To accomp——!" the rancher spat out.

"Yes," agreed de Martin. "If you will join us, I can explain over supper."

"I invited you first," Goodnight pointed out. "It won't be anything fancy——"

"We'll be delighted to accept," de Martin said. "My sister is not the world's best cook—if you know what I mean."

"I'll be gallant and say 'no,'" Goodnight smiled. "Rowdy's food is plain, but well cooked."

"Then perhaps we can add a little comfort of our own?" the newcomer answered, also smiling. "We have a table, chairs, a few tolerable wines. Why be uncomfortable when a few luxuries weigh so little extra?"

Knowing that to deviate might cause resentment, Goodnight always lived and ate at the same standard as his men when on the trail. However he could see no harm in accepting de Martin's offer as it would only happen once. During the meal, he intended to show the newcomers the impossibility of their accompanying the drive.

"My thanks for your offer," the rancher said. "And I gratefully accept."

"We have a table and a few other things in the wagon, gentlemen," Barbe called, looking around the camp. "If I could have——"

"I'll see to it," Dawn put in, before another rush could commence.

"Lend her a hand, Turkey, Boiler," Mark confirmed, selecting fast. The cook's louse was an unprepossessing young man and the grizzled oldtimer's interest in women had been tempered by years of experience. "The rest of you stay put."

Although Mark had an eye for a beautiful woman and was anything but averse to female company under the right conditions,* he saw the danger of allowing the men

---

*This is proved in *The Wildcats* and *Troubled Range*.

to compete for the favors—small though they might be—of the newly arrived girl. So he held down his own impulse to go and help, giving the chore to the men he felt most suitable to handle it. Before the drive it had been decided that Mark would take over as segundo in Dusty's absence, so nobody questioned his right to give the orders.

Clearly the de Martin family believed in traveling comfortably. Looking at the interior of the wagon, Mark smiled a little. There was a wide, well-padded bed fastened to the front end and the rest of the space held a variety of boxes and trunks. Barbe pointed out a small collapsible table and three folding chairs, fussing over her male helpers until they had removed and set them up. Then she opened boxes to produce a fancy candelabra, plates, cutlery and wine glasses.

While setting out the table, Barbe more or less ignored Dawn. Nor did the western girl show a greater inclination to offering friendship. Turning, Barbe started to walk by the end of the wagon toward the darkness beyond it. As if struck by a thought, she stopped and looked back.

"Er—Miss—I—I want to——" Barbe spluttered, dropping her eyes with becoming modesty to avoid the men's gaze.

"Come on then," Dawn replied. "I want to go myself."

"I suppose you have lost all your clothes and have had to borrow those—garments?" Barbe remarked as they walked away from the camp.

"Nope," Dawn answered. "I'm working on the drive, and they're better'n fancy do-dads for handling cattle. Say. Did the dressmaker run out of cloth, or have you grown some since you bought that frock?"

Barbe swung her head sharply in Dawn's direction, fluttering a hand to the exposed upper section of her bust, but read only bland innocence on the other's face. Giving a low sniff, she flounced ahead and Dawn followed, grinning slightly. In Dawn's opinion, their first clash could be called a draw.

When the girls returned, they found Goodnight and de Martin waiting by the table. Refusing an invitation to join them, Dawn continued to walk toward the fire. She arrived in time to hear Heenan describing what "that fancy French gal" wore beneath her gown. One of the listeners remarked, as Dawn came up, that Heenan appeared to be remarkably well informed. A sly grin came to the hardcase's face and he explained that there was a small slit in the wagon's canopy which offered a view of the interior.

"When she's getting undressed——" Heenan began, rolling his eyes ecstatically and chopped off his words as he became aware of the girl's presence.

"I'll put rock-salt into *anybody* I see sneaking around that wagon after she's got into it," Dawn announced grimly.

"And I'll load the gun for her," Mark went on. "Only it won't be needed. As soon as I tell her brother, he'll have that slit covered over."

Taking in the great spread of the blond giant's shoulders and the way the ivory-handled Colts flared so perfectly in their holsters, Heenan held back the comment which had started to rise. Not until Mark walked away accompanied by the hands he selected for the first spell of picket duty did the man make his views known.

"I never figured Cap'n Fog'd be a spoilsport."

"That's Mark Counter, not Cap'n Fog," Vern told Heenan.

"Only, was I you," Billy Jack went on. "I'd mind what he said."

Goodnight enjoyed the meal, finding Barbe's presence pleasant and decorative while her brother was a sparkling conversationalist. For all that, the rancher was not sorry when the girl said that she would retire for the night and rose. He wanted to talk with de Martin about returning to wherever they came from.

Seeing the other girl going to the wagon, Dawn made a decision. Mark had not spoken with the rancher about Heenan's comments, so Dawn went over to the table.

"Well I'll be——!" Goodnight growled as the girl delivered her news.

"So will I," de Martin went on, a flicker of annoyance

crossing his handsome face. "Leave it to me, I will attend to the matter straight away."

"I hope I done the right thing, Colonel," Dawn said worriedly. "I don't go much on running to the boss and telling tales."

"You did right," Goodnight confirmed. "If those fools'd've tried to sneak a look at Miss de Martin, there could have been trouble."

"Figured there might be," Dawn admitted. "They'd likely've started fighting for who got the best place to look from. *Men!*"

"I've attended to it, Charles," de Martin announced, dropping from the wagon after Dawn had returned to the fire. "That damned Heenan—still, he got me to you. And you're probably wondering what a dude like me can possibly want that I should follow you all the way from Young County, and ask to accompany you to Fort Sumner."

"The notion *had* crossed my mind," Goodnight admitted, accepting the cigar de Martin offered.

"It's simple. I'm a photographic artist, a good one if I say so myself, and have been commissioned by General Vindfallet to go to Fort Sumner to produce illustrations for a book he is writing about life on the western frontier."

"That figures, knowing Vindfallet; him writing a book, I mean."

"The General isn't entirely unaware of its value socially," de Martin smiled. "And, as I have a certain reputation in my line, he contacted me. I must admit that I was dubious at first. But he suggested that I should join and accompany you. He also promised to write and inform you of our coming."

"I never had any letter from him!" Goodnight stated.

"Probably it was lost in the mails," de Martin suggested. "He seemed so confident it would be all right that I made no other arrangements. Then, when I reached your ranch, after an unavoidable delay, I found that you had already left. Heenan had escorted us that far and said that we could easily catch up with you, so we came along."

"I'm sorry——" Goodnight began.

"I realize that it is something of an imposition, Charles. More so in view of Vindfallet's letter not arriving. But my professional reputation depends on my completing this commission. So I am determined to do so at all costs. Even if it means completing the journey alone and with Heenan as my guide."

"You don't know what you're saying. If you've any sense, you'll turn around and take your sister back East."

"That isn't possible. Barbe won't agree. You see, I must go to Fort Sumner and we have no kinfolk. There is a certain man forcing his attentions on her and if she was left alone, unprotected—You understand?"

"Yes. But——"

"I don't see why she can't come along. You have that young lady with you."

"Dawn Sutherland was born out here and knows what she's facing."

"My mind is made up, Charles!" de Martin declared. "My sister and I go on, with or without you. I say now that I understand your objections and hold you no ill will if you refuse to take us, for you must have the best of reasons not to. But if we try it alone and are killed, there will be those who say you are responsible for our deaths."

Annoyance flickered across the rancher's face as he thought of the position General Vindfallet had placed him in. If the rancher refused to take the de Martins, his men would certainly protest. Some of them might even consider the only right response would be to escort the brother and sister. Even if Goodnight persuaded the cowhands to change their minds, he would have a worried, discontented crew.

Yet he could hardly take a delicate, well-bred and beautiful city woman over the hell of the Staked Plains. Nor, equally certain, could he turn Barbe and her brother loose to fend for themselves. In addition to all the other hazards on the way to Fort Sumner, Heenan would be a mighty bad choice for a guide. Already he had spied on Barbe and apparently could not wait to start boasting of it. At the first hint of danger, he would probably desert the couple. Or, when certain it could be done safely, kill the brother and do far worse to the sister.

"All right," Goodnight said grimly. "I'll take you along—but on my terms."

"They are?" de Martin asked.

"First that you sign the same Articles of Agreement as the rest of the crew. Second, that you and your sister obey without question all orders given by me or my segundo."

"Accepted, and I'm sure Heenan will agree also."

"Heenan?"

"He's going to Fort Sumner to enlist in the Army for reasons I have not questioned, but seem pressing. As he came with me instead of going north and joining an Army supply convoy, I feel a certain responsibility for him."

"He can stay," Goodnight grunted.

"I will keep him in my employment, he helps attend to the wagon and does other such work for me."

"Like I said," Goodnight answered. "He can go along, as long as he signs and sticks to my conditions."

"I'm sure he will."

"One more thing, Edmond. Would you ask your sister to wear something less—revealing. Those men of mine have enough on their minds without——You understand?"

"I do. And I'll mention it to her in the morning."

"If you want, I'll ask Dawn to sleep in the wagon with your sister," Goodnight offered.

"Doesn't she have duties with the herd?"

"She rides her spell on night herd, but I can leave her off it."

"That won't be necessary. We'll be in your camp area and I'm sure I can rely on the behavior of your men."

"You can!" the rancher said stiffly. "Now, much as I hate breaking up this pleasant evening, I've things to do."

On Mark's return from setting out the pickets, Goodnight told him that the de Martins would be accompanying the drive.

"Across——!" the blond giant began, then closed his mouth before making any reference to the Staked Plains.

"All the way," agreed Goodnight. "De Martin's set on getting there and stubborn enough to try it with Heenan for a guide——"

The sound of approaching hooves chopped off further conversation. From the direction they came, the riders might be the first part of the night guard returning. Yet they were pushing their horses at speed, and that could mean trouble. Mark and Goodnight tensed slightly, hands straying gunward. Then they relaxed. Instead of coming straight into camp, as would be the case if they brought bad news, the riders halted at the remuda. Soon after, the first of them appeared. Carrying his saddle and striding out fast, Burle Willock darted expectant glances around as he made for his bedroll.

"Where's she at?" the cowhand demanded. "We heard tell that there's a right pretty lil city gal around here."

"There for sure is," Jacko Lefors informed him. "Ain't she something to see, boys? Got apples on her the size of melons and ain't scared of showing them around."

Mark scowled, realizing what had happened. Hearing about the de Martins from their reliefs, the younger members of the first watch had made a fast ride in to see Barbe. They had, at least, shown sufficient good sense to leave their horses at the remuda instead of galloping straight up to the fire. Then Mark saw the red flush on Dawn's cheeks and moved toward her.

"Some of you should wash your mouths out with soapy water!" the girl snorted.

"What's up, Dawn gal?" Willock sneered, grinning wolfishly. "Getting jealous 'cause we don't say things like that about you?"

"Anybody who did'd right soon answer to me for it!" Vern snapped.

"And I'll be stood at his side on it," Narth went on.

"Josh, go help Heenan there with de Martin's horses!" Goodnight growled before more could be said. "Vern, help Rowdy check up on the ammunition. And all of you hear me good. Those folks're coming with us to Fort Sumner. They're *my* guests. I'm saying no more than that."

It was enough apparently, for the subject of Barbe's attractions was dropped. Although Dawn almost mirrored Mark's reactions to the news, she said nothing.

"Mark," Goodnight said, leading the way from the fire and beyond the crew's hearing. "We'll have to do something about that girl. Those fool young hands'll be swarming around her like bees to honey——Unless they figure that she's spoke for by you."

"Spoke for?"

"Damn it! I shouldn't have to explain *that* to one of Big Rance Counter's sons. I want for you to make it look like Miss Barbe and you're real close friends. And I don't reckon any of them, even Austin, Vern or Willock'd be *loco* enough to lock horns with you over her."

A slow grin crept on to Mark's face as he considered Goodnight's words and their implications. Since the drive had commenced, the hands had seen sufficient examples of the blond giant's exceptional strength to be fully aware of his potential. So he was ideally suited to carry out the rancher's orders.

"I'll give it a whirl, sir," Mark promised. "Now don't that go to prove what a loyal hand I am, making a sacrifice like that?"

"Remind yourself *not* to ask for a bonus for doing it," Goodnight answered dryly.

CHAPTER NINE

He Must be Burle Willock's Kin

"Indians coming, Colonel Charlie," announced Billy Jack with almost gloomy satisfaction as he rode to where the rancher was sitting on a knoll ahead of the trail herd.

Not wanting to give the hands time to think about the newcomers, Goodnight had insisted on getting the herd moving in the usual manner on the morning after the de Martins' arrival. Before Barbe had made her appearance, much to their disappointment, the cowhands had been taken out to the herd. There Goodnight had given them orders which temporarily drove all thoughts of the girl from their heads. Faced with the possibility of an Indian attack, even the three men Goodnight had named the previous night had enough good sense to concentrate on the business in hand.

It was almost noon, with the cattle continuing to move westward. Sent ahead to act as scout in the Kid's absence, Billy Jack had just returned to report on his findings. Galloping from the point, Mark reined in his horse and looked to the rancher for orders.

"Throw the herd off the trail!" Goodnight said. "Signal to the drag men to drop back to the wagons, then you and Swede get your men up on the point."

"Yo!" Mark replied, turning his horse and riding away.

After the cattle's forward progress had ceased, Goodnight watched the trail hands taking up their alotted positions. Then the rancher and Billy Jack turned their attention to the distant riders.

"Cap'n Dusty 'n' the Kid's with 'em," Billy Jack commented, relief plain in his voice.

Even as the lanky cowhand spoke, the Kid rode ahead of the others and stopped his white stallion. Raising his rifle into the air with his right hand, he put his left up as if to shield his eyes from the glare of the sun, then indicated the men behind him.

"He wants us to show the Indians our rifles when they come." Goodnight translated. "Best do it, I reckon. Fog back and tell the men I said it's all right for them to let the Comanches look, but that none of them have to do anything that might spark off trouble."

"I'll warn 'em good," Billy Jack promised.

Left alone almost a quarter of a mile in front of the herd, Goodnight watched and waited for the Indians to arrive. A more prudent, or less knowledgeable man would have taken off the jaguar-skin vest that had become so well known to the *Nemenuh*. Wise in Indian ways, Goodnight did no such thing. The Comanche admired a brave man, even if he might be an enemy, and would feel the more respect if they saw he did not fear to let them know he was *Chaqueta-Tigre* who had caused their people grief on occasion.

"How!" Goodnight greeted as the Comanches halted and their chief accompanied Dusty and the Kid forward to where the rancher waited.

"How!" the chief answered.

"This's *Pinedapoi*, chief of the *Yamparikuh* and his *hunters*, Colonel," introduced the Kid, laying emphasis on the next-to-last word. "*Pinedapoi*, this's *Chaqueta-Tigre*. The chief has come to see the guns-which-shoot-many-times."

"Take him to look at them," Goodnight offered, also speaking the Comanche tongue but using the dialect of the *Tanima*, Liver-Eater, band with which he was most familiar. He could guess at the reason for the request and willingly gave his permission. Then he turned to Dusty, "How did it go?"

"Easy enough in the end. Lon showed them how a Henry can pour out lead, and be reloaded as you shoot. After that it was just dickering."

One of the improvements to the "New Model Henry" was that it could be loaded through a slot in the frame instead of following the old, slower way of retracting the spring and opening the entire tube on hinges. With the new rifle, one could load and fire in the manner of a single-shot, but still retain a full magazine of sixteen rounds against an emergency. As Dusty claimed the Comanches had seen the advantage of the improvement and been much impressed.

"We can go through then?" asked the rancher.

"Yes. I've offered them six good horses and a dozen head from the herd. It's to show our hearts're good, not a tribute."

A subtle difference which Goodnight understood. Passing through another hunting party's area, Indian braves would share their meat as a sign of good faith. But, if strong enough to enforce their will, they did it voluntarily. Tribute implied that the people giving it had no other choice. The *Yamparikuh* would be less inclined to make trouble with "good heart" givers than for people who paid tribute.

Hearing a noise behind them, Dusty and Goodnight looked around. One of the braves rode from among the *Yamparikuh* and stared at the cattle. Taller and heavier than the majority of his companions, he had an air of truculence about him. Dressed in the style of a dandified, successful young warrior, he carried a war-axe and long-bladed knife balancing themselves on his belt and was one of the few firearms' owners. Judging by the scalp of long, lank black hair which decorated his knife's sheath, he had met with victory on a previous mission.

Holding a tack-decorated Mississippi rifle in his right hand, he pointed toward the herd with his left and made an explosive comment to his companions.

"Damn it!" Goodnight growled, *sotto voce* to Dusty. "He's seen Buffalo and allows that'll be the wohaw he takes from us."

For his part, Dusty had already identified the brave as Apache's Scalp, a *tuivitsi* approaching the status of *tehnap*. He had been the man who directed the *Comancheros* to the camp, and had returned with his companions shortly before the party set out to meet the herd that morning. The small Texan had liked little he had seen of Apache's Scalp so far; and the suggestion did nothing to change his feelings.

"The hell he does!" Dusty breathed. "I can't see the crew parting with ole Buffalo, can you?"

"No," admitted Goodnight. "We'd best see what the Kid has to say about it."

Since assuming its post as lead steer, Buffalo had become very popular with the crew. Calm, intelligent, with none of the vicious traits which so many of its kind possessed, Buffalo had led the herd and proved invaluable. Losing it, even if the trail hands allowed that to happen, would mean that the rest of the cattle would be disturbed until a new leader asserted itself. So Dusty knew that they faced a tricky situation and started to think how it might be averted.

Going to where the right flank's party waited, *Pinedapoi* saw the repeating rifles held by some of its members. The Kid had one of them work the lever of his Spencer carbine to eject bullets, then display the remainder of its load by opening the magazine in its butt. However, having examined León's weapon, the chief already knew that it would be capable of a rate of fire almost as fast as that of the Henry. With the first inspection over, they rode on in the direction of the wagons and remuda in its rope corral.

Following the orders delivered by Billy Jack, Red Blaze had all his party formed up before the wagons. In the rear of the men stood Barbe, wearing a more demure dress than on her arrival, and Dawn, gripping her shotgun. De Martin was at Red's right side, holding a Sharps breech-loading rifle. To Red's left, Heenan had his right hand thumb-hooked close to the butt of his revolver.

"What's that stinking red varmint want?" Heenan demanded.

"Don't ask me," Red replied, Spencer carbine hanging at arm's length in both hands. "All of you mind what I say. No shooting unless I give the word."

"Some of us might be a mite choosier 'n you about having stinking Injuns rub hoss-droppings in our faces," Heenan growled. "If it'd've been me, I'd've started throwing lead as soon as they come into range."

"You're not handling things, *hombre*," Red reminded him. "So you just stand fast and do like I told you."

"I'll think on it," Heenan promised, his hand crawling around toward and fingers gripping the Colt's butt.

Alert for any trouble, Red had been watching Heenan from the corner of his eye. Suddenly he swung his arms forward and propelled the carbine aroundso that its metal-shod butt crashed with some force into Heenan's groin. With a croaking yelp, the man removed his hand hurriedly from the Colt and clutched at the stricken area. Buckling at the knees, he collapsed to the ground where he lay moaning in agony.

"You just stay down there," Red ordered. "If you didn't mean to draw, I'll apologize most humble later on."

"What's the idea?" de Martin hissed, staring at the writhing hardcase.

"If that damned fool'd pulled and started shooting, we'd be up to our knees from the neck down with riled-up Comanches," Red answered. "Which, with your sister along, I don't reckon you'd want to happen."

If the chief had noticed the incident—and he could hardly have missed it—he regarded Red's actions as a sign of good faith. After studying the various weapons, *Pinedapoi* passed on in the direction of the third and final party. Pushing away from the wagon against which she had been standing, Barbe stormed up to Red.

"Why did you hit him?" she hissed.

"To stop him getting us all killed, ma'am," Red replied. "It seemed like a good thing to do at the time—and still does."

"Mr. Blaze acted correctly, my dear," de Martin went on. "Heenan acted in a foolish manner and might have endangered all our lives."

"Get him to the wagon, two of you," Red ordered. "And tell him if he's any complaints to come and see me."

Although the message was delivered, Heenan declined the offer. He scowled whenever he saw Red, but made no attempt at taking reprisals.

After seeing the number of men armed with repeating rifles or carbines, *Pinedapoi* realized the wisdom of accepting the "good heart" gifts. The main body of the *Yamparikuh* band had split into a number of family or clan groups and scattered in search of horses and hunting. Any force less than the band's full fighting strength would meet crippling losses or be completely wiped out facing so many guns-which-fire-many-times in the hands of the calm, clearly competent Texas ride-plenties. Accepting the gifts would save *Pinedapoi* from losing face or authority when the story was told. The Comanches admired bravery, but knew the difference between it and life-wasting stupidity.

"Take our gifts and we leave the white brother in peace!" the chief ordered on rejoining his men.

"I want the wohaw that looks like a buffalo," announced Apache's Scalp.

"No!" Dusty snapped, guessing what the young buck was saying when he heard the word "wohaw."

That was the name Indians gave to cattle, being derived from the commands "whoa" and "haw" used by bullwhackers to guide their draught oxen.

"You won't let us have our gifts?" asked *Pinedapoi*, brows knitting ominously.

"Not the one that looks like a buffalo," Dusty replied.

At Dusty's side, the Kid tensed slightly. Dressed once more in his cowhand's clothing, he looked young and innocent—but as ready for action as a cougar crouching to attack.

"Apache's Scalp says that he wants that wohaw," the

chief pointed out, sounding just a touch uneasy. "He has a strong head for it."

"No!" Dusty repeated and saw the *Yamparikuh* fingering their weapons. "It's my medicine animal."

Instantly the hostile gestures came to a halt. Dusty's words had put his refusal in a light the Indians understood. No man, especially a warrior of Magic Hands' standing, would allow his medicine animal—a bringer of good luck—to be taken from him. Just as the small Texan had expected, Apache's Scalp intended to force the issue. The *tuivitsi* was at an age when he wanted to prove himself the toughest and boldest brave-heart ever born. Although he had heard the story of the Devil Gun council, and about the fight with the *Comancheros*, the young buck chose to regard both as fabrications. Such a small man, white at that, could not be capable of a warrior's deeds. Combined with his natural truculence and dislike of all palefaces, Apache's Scalp was marching straight into the trap laid for him by Dusty.

"I am going to take the wohaw anyway!" the *tuivitsi* announced and the Kid translated the words. He slapped a hand on the hair dangling from his knife's sheath and continued, "Think well before you try to stop me, small white one. This is the scalp of an Apache I wear."

To the Comanche, taking an Apache's scalp ranked high among a warrior's deeds. In the case of the savage warriors from the desert country, the old saying, "Anybody can scalp a dead man" did not apply. A brave who killed an Apache considered he had done very well and wanted people to be aware of the fact.

"He was a deaf Apache," Dusty scoffed, with the Kid for his interpreter. "With age in his bones and no sight in his eyes."

Snarling in rage, Apache's Scalp made as if to raise his rifle. Three-quarters of a second later, he looked down the muzzle of Dusty's left hand Colt and wondered how it came to be lined on him. With his usual speed, Dusty had drawn and cocked the gun at the other's first hostile movement. The small Texan sat holding the *tuivitsi*'s life in his hands.

"Throw away the rifle!" Dusty ordered.

"It's for you to choose," the Kid warned after delivering the command.

Slowly, with every evidence of sullen reluctance, Apache's Scalp flung his rifle aside. Dusty felt a touch of relief, for he had not wished to kill the brave. However, he knew that a stronger lesson might be needed to settle Apache's Scalp and prepared to give it. Backing off his paint stallion, Dusty holstered the Colt. Before the *tuivitsi* could decide what to do, Dusty tossed his right leg across the saddlehorn and jumped clear of the horse. Never taking his eyes from Apache's Scalp, he unbuckled and removed his gunbelt to hang it on the paint's saddle.

"Tell him the buffalo-wohaw gives me real big medicine, Lon," Dusty ordered. "So much that I don't need weapons to handle a *tuivitsi*. Then tell him that if he still figures to take my medicine to come right ahead and try it."

Apache's Scalp listened to the words with growing disbelief and fury. Then he flung back his head and let out a roaring curse.

"He must be Burle Willock's kin," The Kid remarked disgustedly to Goodnight as the brave sprang from his horse. "That much stupidness runs in families."

"Soon I have a white man's scalp to wrap around my war-axe!" screeched Apache's Scalp and snatched that weapon from his belt.

"This is between the two of them, *Chaqueta-Tigre?*" asked *Pinedapoi*.

"It is," Goodnight confirmed and raised his voice in a bellow as he saw some of the cowhands moving restlessly. "Nobody interferes. Mark. Swede. Shoot down any man who tries to use his gun."

"Reckon them Injuns'll stay out of it?" Willock muttered as he sat at Mark's side.

"As long as we do," the blond giant answered. "Which we're going to, even if I have to do what Colonel Charlie told me."

Advancing with his war-axe ready, Apache's Scalp became aware of the change in his opponent. No longer did the ride-plenty look small, but was big, powerful and dangerous. Maybe there was truth in his words and he did gain medicine power from the buffalo-wohaw.

Balancing lightly on the balls of his feet, Dusty watched the Comanche closing in on him. From all appearances, Apache's Scalp had been well taught and handled the war-axe efficiently. Yet Dusty also figured that the *tuivitsi* would be reckless, proud of his skill and likely to act in a rash manner should things go wrong.

Which was what Dusty intended would happen.

Across and up lashed the war-axe's blade, but Dusty took a step to the rear and carried himself beyond the arc of its two-foot handle. Swiftly, with little loss of momentum, the brave reversed direction, chopping savagely across. Again he missed as Dusty avoided the blow. Going forward with the force of it, he was carried past the small Texan who slammed a quickly snapped side-kick to his ribs in passing. Apache's Scalp stumbled, caught his balance and whirled fast as Dusty moved toward him.

Snarling in fury, the *tuivitsi* attacked. Time after time the deadly axe, its edge as sharp as many a barber's razor, licked in Dusty's direction and met only empty air. The blows became wilder, less well timed as their maker's rage and frustration increased. Watching every move, Dusty figured that he could lure his attacker into some ill-advised move and where he could bring the fight to an end. The spectators on both sides were getting more excited by the second. Yells of encouragement rang out in English and Comanche, but so far neither side showed any sign of objecting to the other's presence. Which was one of the reasons Dusty wanted to terminate the affair quickly.

By what seemed to be an accident, Dusty slipped in the course of evading a slash. Out shot the Comanche's left hand to catch hold of Dusty's shirt at its open neck. With a screech of triumph, Apache's Scalp swung up his other hand and prepared to drive the axe into the Texan's skull. It seemed that nothing could save Dusty. Certainly the *tuivitsi* knew of no way in which his intended victim might escape.

Which, unfortunately for him, was not the sum lack of Apache's Scalp's knowledge. He did not know about the small Oriental who worked in the Rio Hondo country as Ole Devil Hardin's personal attendant. Nobody could say what caused Tommy Okasi to flee his native Japanese islands, for he never mentioned the subject. No matter why he left, he brought along a thorough education in his country's unarmed fighting skills. More than that, he had passed on to the smallest male member of the Hardin-Fog-Blaze clan the secrets of *ju-jitsu* and *karate*. With such knowledge, virtually unknown outside the Orient at that time, backing his powerful muscular development, Dusty could deal with men of greater weight and superior strength. The Ignorance was to cost Apache's Scalp dearly.

Startled yells rose from the watching trail hands, mingled with Mark's and Ahlén's demands that orders were obeyed. Throwing up his hands inside the *tuivitsi*'s left arm, Dusty crossed his wrists and interposed them between the down-driving war-axe and his head. Caught in the upper V formed by the wrists, Apache's Scalp's forearm halted without achieving its purpose.

Before the *tuivitsi* realized the danger, Dusty slipped free his right hand to grasp the immobile wrist. Pulling it forward and downward, the small Texan twisted himself to the right. Taking a rearward step with his right foot, Dusty hauled even harder on the trapped limb and pivoted on his left leg to drag Apache's Scalp off balance. Giving the other no chance to recover, Dusty propelled his right knee around to drive it into the exposed and offered belly.

An agony-filled belch broke from the *tuivitsi*'s lips as the knee arrived. Having withdrawn his left hand from the X-block position when the right gripped Apache's Scalp's wrist, Dusty knotted it into a fist which he drove with all his power just below the other's rib-cage. Dropping the axe, the *tuivitsi* blundered by Dusty on being released and fell to his knees.

Dusty followed his victim grimly. Although they watched with considerable interest and commented excitedly among themselves, none of the *Yamparikuh* braves offered to intervene. Going against another man's declared medicine power, Apache's Scalp must stand or fall alone. Despite their lack of interference, Dusty knew he must end the fight quickly.

Raising his right arm, Dusty kept the hand open, its fingers extended and thumb bent across the palm. Down it whipped and he slashed the heel of the hand into the side of the *tuivitsi's* neck above the vagus nerve. Apache's Scalp stiffened as the blow landed, then collapsed limply forward. Rolling him on to his back, Dusty bent and took the knife from its scalp-decorated sheath. Amazement showed on the *Yamparikuh* faces as the small Texan walked toward them. Springing from their horses, two of the *tuivitsi* ran by him in the direction of their motionless companion.

"Is that one dead?" asked *Pinedapoi* as Dusty offered him the knife, hilt first.

"No. He will wake soon," the small Texan answered. "Does any other want to take the buffalo-wohaw?"

Although he could not understand the majority of grunted answers, Dusty concluded that they expressed a complete disinterest in gaining possession of his medicine animal. Discovering that Dusty had spoken the truth about Apache's Scalp's condition, *Pinedapoi* stated his complete satisfaction. Nor did Apache's Scalp show any inclination to resume his demands, having received what he regarded as convincing proof of the medicine's capabilities. So, with a further exchange of compliments, the *Yamparikuh* departed taking their "good heart" gifts.

"They'll not trouble us any more," the Kid stated. "Especially with you giving *Pinedapoi* that extra hoss and three head."

The bonus had been handed over by Goodnight as a compliment to a wise and brave *Nemenuh* chief. It was the kind of gesture Indians liked and would increase *Pinedapoi's* determination to keep his promise of peaceful passage for the herd.

Not until the herd had been started moving did the Kid realize that he had failed to satisfy his curiosity on a certain point.

"Say, Colonel. Who's the dude and that fancy gal back with the wagons?"

CHAPTER TEN
You Could Lose the Whole Damned Herd

"And if she takes to Mark, which I reckon she might, we shouldn't have any trouble over her," Goodnight concluded after explaining to his segundo and scout about the de Martins' presence.

"Could be," Dusty agreed. "The only fellers big enough to make fuss for him are Swede, Sherm Sherman or Tod Ames and they're old enough 'n' steady enough not to try it."

"It all depends on the gal, though," warned the Kid. "Women're mighty peculiar critters."

During the next three days, Barbe de Martin seemed determined to prove false the Kid's views on female peculiarity. While the younger hands swarmed about her on the first morning, trying to attract her attention with displays of roping or riding skill, they kept their distance once Mark made his intentions plain. No mean hand at the flirting game, and possessed of the attributes most likely to attract women—handsome face, magnificent physique and wealth—he found little difficulty in drawing Barbe to him.

The situation lasted only three days. On the evening of the third, Mark and Barbe were walking in a small valley clear of the camp. He had already found her to be a lot freer with her favors than expected and had wondered if maybe the man back East was the one doing the forcing. However, instead of flying into his arms at the first opportunity, she acted hesitant. A low gasp broke from her as he slipped an arm around her waist.

"What's wrong?" he asked as she drew away from him and clapped a hand to her side, face showing pain.

"I—I fell and banged myself in the wagon this afternoon," Barbe replied.

"Is it hurting bad?"

"No. But you pressed it and it stung. Mark——"

"Yes?"

"Nothing can come of our friendship, can it?"

"How do you mean, nothing?" Mark asked warily.

"I mean when we get to Fort Sumner, you'll go your way and I'll go mine," Barbe explained.

"It's likely," Mark admitted.

"It's certain," she smiled. "I've seen you with your friends. You wouldn't leave them to come East and live. And I couldn't stay in this wild land. So nothing can come of our friendship, can it?"

"Likely not. But it's real pleasant."

"It's *too* pleasant," Barbe said, darting a glance around her. "Mark, you wouldn't marry me. Would you?"

"I reckon you're going just a touch too fast," Mark answered. "We've not known each other——"

"You wouldn't," Barbe sniffed. "So I think that it is better we end this now. You would be too easy to fall in love with, Mark. Neither of us want that, do we?"

"Maybe not."

"I could too easily find myself deeply involved, Mark. So we must stop doing this. We must."

A slight sound reached Mark's ears, coming from some bushes about thirty yards away. Gently thrusting the girl from him, the blond giant faced them and his right hand Colt flowed from its holster in the effortless-seeming, yet lightning-fast way which separated the expert from the average in the *pistolero* arts.

"Don't shoot, Mark!" called de Martin's voice and he walked into view with a shotgun tucked under his arm. "I was walking and heard voices, so I came over to see who it was."

"Edmond!" Barbe said, sounding startled. "I—I was just talking with Mark about the matter we discussed this evening."

"And does he agree?"

"We understand each other. Don't we, Mark?"

"I reckon so," Mark replied, holstering his Colt.

"If I thought it would work and Barbe be happy, I would be the first to say 'Go ahead Mark,' de Martin stated. "But, as her elder brother, I was naturally concerned. I've nothing against you personally, and feel that you would have been a suitable choice. But Barbe is a city girl. She could not settle in this land and I doubt if you would like living in the East. Come, Barbe. We'll go back to the camp."

Watching the brother and sister fade off into the darkness, Mark felt as if a cold hand had touched him. The way things sounded, he had been under consideration as a matrimonial prospect and had only narrowly avoided acceptance in that light.

"Whooee!" the blond giant breathed, mopping his brow with a bandana. "Mark boy, you've got to stop being a loyal hand making sacrifices happen you get asked to handle another chore like that."

"They do say the first sign's when they start talking to themselves?" drawled the Kid's voice.

Spinning around with hands driving to his guns, Mark halted the draw uncompleted and glared indignantly at the dark youngster who materialized from the darkness. Familiarity did not lessen the surprise the Kid could hand out when he made one of his silent appearances.

"Blast you, you danged *Pehnane*!" Mark spat out, letting the revolvers return to leather. "I near on killed you, jumpy as I am over that narrow escape I've just had."

"It was narrower than you think," the Kid replied. "Her brother was hid up behind that bush, listening to every word you said."

"The hell you say!" Mark growled.

"Left camp just after you did, toting his shotgun. I thought he might be fixing to do some hunting and tagged along. When I saw his game, I waited unknown to him. Figured maybe you'd like to have a witness on hand."

"Thanks, Lon. I reckon they'd fixed together to have Barbe break off with me and Edmond come along in case I'd got notions to the contrary. Let's get back to camp and tell Dusty what's happened."

On hearing of the incident, Dusty agreed with Mark's ideas about de Martin's motives and that there would be no point in the blond giant continuing his efforts. If he attempted to carry the matter further, the other hands might consider that he was trying to force unwanted attentions on the girl. Figuring that and wanting to raise his standing in Barbe's eyes, one of the impressionable young men might intervene. Which would spark off just what Goodnight was seeking to avoid.

So, although Barbe threw yearning or even inviting glances his way, Mark made no further attempt to resume their close acquaintance. Seeing his attitude, the younger hands swarmed in like hounds around a coon on a tree stump. In the main, the competition was shared between Vern Sutherland, Austin Hoffman and Burle Willock, with Jacko Lefors trailing along out of deference for the latter. By careful manipulation of their duties, Dusty made sure that the trio only rarely found themselves in camp at the same time. Barbe also showed interest in Red Blaze, but achieved nothing. Being aware of Mark's narrow escape, Red figured the girl might consider him a matrimonial prospect. There were two things scared Red: being left afoot and the risk of being tricked into marriage. So he steered clear of Barbe.

If his sister mingled with the younger hands, although ignoring Dawn, de Martin gained the confidence and friendship of the older, staider members of the traveling community. He had knowledge, was willing to listen and learn, so got on well with the senior trail hands. As the drive continued, he used his photographic equipment to gather material for Vindfallet's book and his own use.

Various members of the crew posed self-consciously before the camera, including a blushing Dawn, and he took long-range pictures of the herd. Goodnight vetoed a suggestion that de Martin should go closer to the cattle as he did not want them disturbed by the blazing fire of magnesium which supplied the necessary light to process the photographic plate.

On went the drive, gathering unbranded—therefore ownerless—cattle which came their way to replace those given to the *Yamparikuh,* used for food, or lost in travelling. Goodnight wanted to keep the size of the herd at around three thousand five hundred head. That would leave him a margin of safety against the crossing of the Staked Plains.

With each passing day, the rancher grew increasingly aware that he must soon tell the crew of his plans. He had noticed that Ahlén, Sherman and Ames in particular had begun to spend time studying the stars at night, or paying extra attention to the route they followed in the daytime. Soon they would start suspecting the continued western course. So he wished to explain his motives before they discovered for themselves which way they were to go.

Black clouds filled the sky as Goodnight left Dusty to handle the bedding-down of the herd. He wanted to make a large circle and check if there was any danger from the approaching storm. On his return to camp, he intended to break the news to the crew.

Satisfied that even a heavy rainfall would cause him no inconvenience, the rancher left his horse with the remuda and walked toward the camp. Immediately he knew something was wrong. Normally the crew, less the herd's guard and night hawk, would be gathered about the fire, eating, making insulting comments about the food or discussing the events of the day. Instead they appeared to be split into three groups. The Swinging G hands and men from the OD Connected's contingent were around Dusty. To the rear of the others, the de Martins and Heenan stood together. With the exception of the D4S trio who had the night herd with Billy Jack, all the Minerals Wells men formed the third party.

"I doubled the night watch, Uncle Charlie," Dusty remarked as the rancher approached him.

Before any more could be said, Ahlén strode over. "What's all this about us taking the herd across the Staked Plains, Colonel?" the big man demanded.

"I'm sorry, Colonel," de Martin called. "I thought that you had told your men the way you intended to go, or I wouldn't have drawn their attention to it on my map."

"Now lookee here, Colonel Charlie," Sherman went on, joining Ahlén. "We've got our bosses' stock to think about and we don't figure to see them killed off."

"Your bosses don't have any stock in this herd," Goodnight said quietly.

A low rumble followed from the Mineral Wells men in echo to the rancher's surprising comments. Ahlén and Sherman exchanged glances, then gave their full attention to Goodnight. Behind them, the rest of their party awaited the next developments. To Dusty's rear, the OD Connected and Swinging G hands stood alert, watchful but in no way openly threatening. It was an explosive situation, calling for the most delicate handling.

"Would you mind making that a mite clearer, Colonel?" Sherman asked, politely enough yet clearly determined to receive an explanation.

"It's simple," Goodnight answered. "Before we left, your bosses signed all their cattle over to me so that I could claim the legal right to sell them at Fort Sumner."

"And you figure we can reach it, Colonel," Ahlén said, "going across the Staked Plains?"

"It's our *only* hope of reaching it in time," Goodnight told him. "Chisum is headed there, going by the trail Oliver Loving and I blazed. He's got almost a week's start on us and we'll never lick him going on his heels. Our only hope is to cross the Staked Plains."

"You could lose the whole damned herd!" Sherman warned.

"It's a chance I'm willing to take," Goodnight assured him.

"You've known about this from the start?" asked Ahlén.

"Since the night the Kid rode in."

"And you didn't mention it to us?"

"I wanted you boys to learn about trail herding first. To let you see what could be done. Well, you've seen and you've learned. If I hadn't faith in you, I'd've turned north after the first week and said to hell with the contract. But I've got faith in you and I say that you boys can take the herd across the Staked Plains if it can be done."

"Does Miss Sutherland know of the route you intended to take?" de Martin asked without leaving his sister's side.

"I told her the first night," Goodnight replied. "Just her. Not her brother, or my hands. She said she wouldn't turn back and I don't reckon she will."

"*We're* going on, anyways!" Dusty put in and the men at his back mumbled their agreement. "The OD Connected and Swinging G don't want it sticking in our craw that Chisum got the better of us."

Dusty spoke deliberately and in a definite challenge, implying that the drive would continue no matter who deserted. No cowhand with loyalty to his brand could mildly allow another outfit to make good on such a boast. Guessing what his cousin had in mind, Red took up the stirring process and continued it.

"I sure wouldn't want it!"

"Maybe it don't mean anything to some folks that Chisum getting there'll be selling their bosses' cattle," Mark carried on from Red's statement.

"Damn it, yes!" Ames growled, slouching forward. "Chisum'll maybe have our cattle along."

"Ain't no 'maybe' about it," drawled the Kid. "He's got 'em."

"In that case, I'm for licking the bald-headed son-of-a-bitch there and taking 'em back when he arrives!" Ahlén growled.

"And me!" Sherman went on, slapping a hand on his thigh. "Whooee! Won't it be a pistol to see his face when he comes and finds us-all waiting."

Once started, agreement to Goodnight's plans came fast and the dangerous tension ebbed away. No cowhand cared to let a rival spread outdo him. Added to that, the idea of beating Chisum to Fort Sumner and retrieving their employers' cattle appealed to their sense of humor or justice.

"There's one thing you gentlemen are forgetting," de Martin announced, walking forward. He brought Barbe with him, an arm draped protectively across her shoulders. "My sister and I are with you. I don't mind the hardships and dangers for myself. But is it fair to risk the life of a beautiful woman?"

Slowly Barbe turned her eyes around the circle of men. On her face was an expression of pleading which begged all the big, strong men to protect her. Although Dusty and Goodnight retained attitudes of stony indifference, they knew that de Martin would gain support.

"Damn it! That wouldn't be right!" Willock declared and was favored by a weak smile of gratitude from Barbe.

"It for sure wouldn't!" Austin went on, not wishing to let a rival gain so much of an advantage over him.

"I warned you that the trip would be dangerous," Goodnight told de Martin.

"But not that you meant to cross the Staked Plains," the photographer replied. "I'm afraid that I can't risk Barbe's life on such a crossing. We will turn north until we find the Army's trail to Fort Sumner."

"Not alone you won't!" Willock declared and the rumble of agreement included members of both the original parties. "Some of us'll come with you."

"What about the herd?" demanded the practical Ahlén.

"Hell! We can easy enough catch up with you after we've seen these folks safe," Willock answered, still basking in Barbe's admiring gaze. "Me 'n' Jacko——"

"I'm going along!" stated Austin grimly.

"What for, to help take pictures of the Comanches killing you off?" interrupted the Kid, for de Martin had been instructing Austin on the use of the camera in order to be photographed with his sister and various members of the crew. "Because, feller, that's what'll happen if you go north from here, or even back east."

"Them Yap-Eaters let us through this far, Kid!" Austin

protested, seeing his chances of a pleasant trip slipping away.

"Only 'cause they didn't have enough men along to do different," the Kid pointed out. "That won't be the way if you pull out. You don't have a chance in a thousand of getting through."

"You reckon so, Kid?" gulped Jacko, impressed by the dark youngster's vehemence and respecting his knowledge of matters Comanche.

"You'd best believe it, happen you want to keep Miss Barbe's scalp from hanging on some *tehnap*'s lodge pole."

"But if you came as our guide, Lon——" de Martin hinted.

"Which I don't aim to, even if it'd help. I took on to ride scout for Colonel Charlie, like these fellers took on to drive the cattle. So I'm keeping my word and doing just that."

Almost instinctively the Kid had said the right thing and struck a nerve among Barbe's protectors. To leave the herd would be betraying their trust and given word. That was something not even irresponsible cusses like Willock, Jacko or Austin wanted to do. Sensing their wavering, Dusty decided to offer them a way out that avoided a loss of face.

"Take it this way, Edmond," he said to de Martin, but making sure his words carried to the trio. "Your only safe bet is to stick with us. But if *you* want to expose Barbe to the danger of being killed—*or worse*—by the Comanches, we'll let these three fellers go along."

That dropped the entire decision into the photographer's lap. If he insisted on going away, it would be his stubbornness which endangered his sister's life. Like Dusty, de Martin could see the uncertainty shown by her champions.

"If you're sure there's danger——" de Martin began.

"I'd take my lodge oath on it," the Kid said with quiet sincerity.

"Then we will accompany you, Charles," the photographer decided.

"It'll not be easy, I won't pretend otherwise,"

Goodnight said. "We'll all be on a strict allowance of water and if it runs short, the horses get first crack at it. That way alone we'll get across alive."

Watching the de Martins, Dusty read nothing on the man's face. However Barbe showed anxiety and seemed to be on the verge of speaking. Her brother swung his head around and she closed her mouth. Swinging on her heel, she stalked toward their wagon and disappeared inside it. Muttering an apology, de Martin followed her.

"Come and get it!" boomed Rowdy with masterly timing, rattling a spoon against his cooking pot. "Come and get it afore I feed it to the other hawgs."

"Come on boys!" Mark yelled. "I'm going to put some fat on afore I start to cross the Staked Plains."

CHAPTER ELEVEN

You Hit Near on as Hard as My Pappy

"That was close!" Dusty breathed as he and Goodnight watched the rush for the chuck wagon.

"Real close," the rancher agreed. "I meant to tell the men about the crossing as soon as I got back tonight. Only it looks I got beat to doing it."

"I'm sorry about that, Uncle Charlie."

"How did it happen?"

"Harmlessly enough. De Martin got talking about how far we've covered and his sister fetched out an Army map. She asked me if I could show her where we're at. I couldn't lie about it with Swede and Sherm there. And as soon's I'd showed her, they knew we weren't on the trail you blazed with Oliver Loving."

"I should have told them earlier," Goodnight declared.

"It all came out right in the end," Dusty answered. "Lucky for us Edmond saw sense. We couldn't've spared those three or four young cusses who aimed to go along with him."

"No," Goodnight agreed. "And they'd've likely been

112

fighting among themselves over Barbe afore they'd gone two miles. It'd've happened before now but for the way you've been keeping them apart. You're doing a good job, Dustine."

"Looks like we'll miss the main storm," Dusty said.

"It's coming heavy up north, for sure," Goodnight replied. "And don't try to change the subject."

"No, sir. Further we go, the more I think we've lost Hayden's men by coming this way."

"I like a segundo as takes orders," smiled Goodnight. "You could be right. Or maybe he figures that seven-day head start had us licked. Tell the Kid to keep watching our back trail regardless."

"I'll see to it," Dusty promised. Then he felt the first patter of rain and went on, "Here it comes. I'll get my fish and ride out to the herd."

Dressed in his yellow oilskin slicker, with the fish picture trademark that produced its name, the small Texan visited the night guard. He found that they had taken warning from the cloud-laden skies and carried protective clothing along. For the first time Billy Jack, Vern and Narth learned of the change in the route, although the former had suspected something of it for a few days. It did, however, furnish him with material for a mournful discourse on their probable fate. While Vern expressed amazement of his "female" sister keeping a secret, Narth took the news more seriously. Yet, such was the faith they had attained in Goodnight and Dusty, that none of them considered the decision unwise, or that it would be other than successfully completed.

Although the trail drive missed passing through the center of the storm, it ran into continuing rain. For a week, with rain falling in varying degrees of severity, the cattle were kept moving westward. In one respect the inclement weather proved a blessing. All the trail hands were kept too busy to brood over Goodnight's failure to inform them of his plans. Nor did the younger hands find time to resume their rivalry. If it came to a point, Barbe did not show to good advantage in the wet weather. Possibly her bedraggled appearance would have evoked sympathy, except that everybody was in the same condition. So Barbe's whining and complaining produced little response other than irritation.

Through all the bad weather, Rowdy and Turkey performed miracles. Every day they managed to produce two hot meals and a plentiful supply of hot coffee for the crew.

At last the rains ended and, as if wishing to make up for the inconvenience, the sun blazed down on the sodden land. Finding an area of reasonably dry ground, Goodnight halted the herd for a day. With the cattle held under the minimum of a guard, the remainder of the party spread out and dried their clothing. Next day the journey was resumed.

Excitement, anticipation and a little concern filled the trail crew when they learned that the South Concho lay only a day's drive ahead. For several days the pace had been slackened and the cattle encouraged to graze on the lush, rich fattening buffalo grass. In the manner of their kind, the steers took advantage of the good feeding and blossomed into top condition. Which was just what the rancher wanted in view of what lay ahead.

"We could push straight on across, sir," Dusty suggested as they watched the herd go by and start spreading on the bed ground appointed for the night. "At dawn, I mean."

"No," Goodnight replied. "They need a rest up to let them take on all the food and water they can. We'll stop here for four days."

"The longer we're here, the more time the crew'll have to think about how tough the crossing's going to be," Dusty warned. "There'll not be much work to keep them occupied while we're in camp."

"A good rest won't do them any harm any more than it will the steers," Goodnight replied and grinned at his nephew. "I reckon *you* can find something to keep them occupied."

"I'll have to," Dusty answered. "If only to keep them from thinking about the Staked Plains—or about Miss Barbe."

"Here's what I'll do, Dustine," the rancher decided.

"I'll take Swede Ahlén, Sherman and one from each of the other Mineral Wells spreads along with me and the Kid on a scout. That'll leave you short-handed enough to keep the rest of 'em busy."

"Sure," Dusty agreed. "Best take Austin along. That'll be one of the rivals out of my hair."

"I could take them all——"

"That'd make it too obvious, sir. Anyways, it'd be best to take men who'll learn something from what they see. I can manage Vern, Jacko and Willock. Austin as well, comes to that."

"I'll take Austin," Goodnight smiled. "You do what you have to for the rest."

With the herd bedded down close to the South Concho, the trail hands gathered for the evening meal. On being told that they would accompany the rancher on his scouting mission, all but Austin agreed that it was a wise precaution. The Swinging G hand saw that his rivals would be left a clear—or reduced—field for Barbe's favors but reluctantly concluded that he must obey orders.

"Sooner them than me!" grinned Vern, heel-squatting by the fire. "All we've got to do here's ride round nice 'n' easy and watch them ole steers getting fatter."

"I sure wish I'd your faith," Dawn told him, darting a glance at Dusty. "Is that all we've got to do?"

"That," Dusty replied and saw relief creep on to various faces. "And a few other lil things."

Listening to Dusty listing all the work he wanted doing, the cowhands lost their relieved expressions. Yet they knew that he was not inventing tasks out of ornery cussedness. Every chore he mentioned needed doing and would increase their chances of safely crossing the Staked Plains. Naturally none of Dusty's audience intended to let their feelings show.

"Would that be all, Cap'n Fog, sir?" Billy Jack asked mildly. "You ain't forgot something now, have you?"

"If he says 'yes,'" Dawn hissed in the lanky cowhand's ear, "I'm going to make all them bad things you're expecting come true."

"They will anyways," Billy Jack replied, after Dusty

had admitted that for the moment he could not think of further tasks. "You see if they don't."

"Anyways," Dawn said. "We can sleep in real late comes morning. Why, Cap'n Dusty says we don't need to roll out until full dawn."

"I'm riding the last watch on night herd," Billy Jack informed her, steadfastly refusing to accept that life held any bright side for him.

Next morning the majority of the trail crew enjoyed their extended spell in bed. Goodnight's party left while the rest ate a leisurely breakfast. Before the men could depart on the tasks assigned to them by Dusty the previous night, Barbe left her wagon. She wore a dainty black Stetson, frilly-fronted white blouse and an Eastern-style riding-skirt. Followed by her brother and Heenan, she crossed to the fire and flashed a dazzling smile at Dusty.

"As we are to be here for a time, I would like to go riding. Could you give me an escort, please, Captain Fog?"

"I'll——!" said at least three eager male voices.

"Dawn'll do it," Dusty interrupted.

"Shouldn't a man go along, Dusty?" de Martin inquired. "Not that I don't trust Dawn, but——"

"It'll be safe enough," Dusty replied. "Don't take Miss de Martin more than a mile from the camp, Dawn. And take along a rifle in case you get a chance to shoot some camp-meat."

"Yo!" Dawn answered. "Come on, gal. I'll pick you a hoss from the remuda."

"Thank you, but Mr. Heenan says I may use his," Barbe replied, a touch coldly. "It is saddled and waiting."

"Come on, it's time some of you started working!" Dusty growled. "Half the day's gone and nothing done. Cousin Red, you're segundo on the herd. Take your crew and let the night herders come in afore Billy Jack starves to death."

"Vern, Jacko, Burle, Spat. Let's go."

Watching Red's section leave, Dusty wondered if he had made the right decision sending the first three out

together. Yet they would be safer away from the camp
than continually thrown into close contact with Barbe in
each other's company. Red and Spat would act as
restraining influences while they handled the comparatively easy work of holding the herd on the eastern banks
of the river.

Although understanding why Dusty had given her the
task, Dawn did not care for it. A friendly-natured girl, she
had tried to be sociable with Barbe on several occasions
and been, if not completely snubbed, shown that the other
girl had no desire for her company. Coming from two
entirely different environments, they had nothing in
common that might have drawn them closer. So, while
willing to carry out her orders, Dawn made little attempt
at conversation as they rode away from the camp.
Concentrating on keeping her seat, Barbe spoke little and
Dawn concentrated upon watching for signs of deer, elk
or pronghorn antelope.

Evidently the presence of the herd had temporarily
driven away the wild animals, for Dawn and Barbe circled
the area and approached where the herd was held without
the western girl seeing anything suitable to shoot for
camp-meat. Dawn made as if to turn away, but Barbe
asked if they could go closer and see the cattle. Not
wishing to appear obstructive, Dawn agreed. As they rode
nearer, Burle Willock saw them and headed in their
direction. Removing his hat with a flourish, the cowhand
bowed over his saddlehorn.

"Howdy, Miss Barbe," he greeted. "It's sure pleasing to
see you out here."

"My! What a tremendous lot of cattle!" Barbe replied,
looking around. "There seem to be so many more when
you see them like this. What do you do if one of them tries
to run away?"

"Turn him back. I can right easy show you."

Before Willock could make good his promise, Vern
came galloping up from the opposite direction and Jacko
rode their way.

"Hey, Miss Barbe!" Vern said, bringing his horse to a
sliding stop.

"Ain't you supposed to be up that ways, watching them draws?" Willock demanded coldly.

"So?" Vern challenged. "You're reckoned to be out on that rim comes to that."

Moving his horse forward, Willock halted it alongside Vern's mount and thrust his face forward grimly. "You get back to what you should be doing, *boy*!"

"Don't you go giving me no orders!" Vern spat back.

"Quit it, the pair of you!" Dawn snapped. "Red's coming——"

"Now you back off, *sonny*!" Willock snarled, drowning the girl's warning. "This time you don't have Dusty Fog on hand to take you p——"

Even as Dawn opened her mouth to repeat the warning, Vern flung himself at Willock. Locked together, they slid sideways from the horse and lit down fighting. Leaping from her saddle, Dawn darted toward the struggling pair.

"Quit it, you fools!" she yelled, trying to separate them as they came to their feet. "Cut i——"

With a surging heave, Willock threw the girl from his arm. She sprawled on to her rump in time to see Vern drive a punch into the other cowhand's face. Sent back a few paces, Willock caught his balance and went into a half-crouch. When Vern charged in recklessly, the more experienced Willock caught him by his vest. Partially trapping the youngsters arms, Willock jerked him closer and butted him between the eyes. Shoving the dazed Vern, Willock sent him reeling to tumble over his sister. Continuing to roll, Vern got clear of Dawn and started to rise. With a grin at Barbe, who sat watching with detached interest, Willock moved forward meaning to hand Vern the beating of his life.

The chance did not come. Having seen the girl's arrival and movement by the cowhands in their direction, Red Blaze wasted no time in making for them. His first intention had been to chase the men back to their work, but the fight gave him a more serious purpose. Maybe Red was a hothead who reveled in fighting, but he never did so at the expense of his duties. So he raced his horse toward the others, ready to end the fight.

Without a glance at Jacko, who had already ridden up and dismounted clear of the combatants, Red quit his running horse and relied on its trailing reins to halt it. On landing, he hurled forward and shoulder-charged Willock. The force of the impact lifted the unsuspecting cowhand from his feet and flung him aside. From doing so, Red pivoted fast to meet the approaching Vern. Lashing around his right arm, Red delivered a backhand blow which sent the youngster spinning. From dealing with Vern, Red started to turn on Willock. What he saw made him put the cowhand out of his thoughts for the moment.

While Jacko was a good cowhand, he was not bright. Loyal to his friends, he regarded Red's treatment of Willock as unreasonable or part of a plot by the D4S to gang up on the Double Two hand. So he rushed to Willock's defense and reached for his Colt. In addition to recognizing his own danger, Red knew that a shot might spook the herd and would certainly provoke a gunfight. So he did not hesitate. Leaping forward as the other tried to clear the revolver from its poorly designed holster, Red kicked him in the groin. Trained from his earliest days to respect firearms and that he must never pull a gun without the intention of using it, Red figured everybody should follow the same rule. Acting on it, he stopped Jacko in a painful, but most effective, manner. Letting out a croak of agony, the cowhand folded over, forgot drawing his Colt and collapsed face down on the grass.

"All right!" Red barked, swinging to face Willock once more. "If you want to fight, get up and try me."

Winded by the charge, Willock shook his head. He knew enough about Red to figure taking him would be far harder and much less certain than licking Vern. So, having no desire to let Barbe see him beaten, Willock declined the offer.

"I—I ain't got no fuss with you, Red. It's betw——"

"Get your hoss and head back to camp!" Red

interrupted. "Tell Dusty to send me three men out here."

"Sure," Willock answered sullenly and obeyed without offering to help the moaning Jacko.

"Whooee!" Vern groaned, standing up and rubbing his cheek. "Red, you hit near on as hard as my pappy——"

"Go watch those draws until somebody comes out to relieve you!" Red snapped. "And if any of the cattle've strayed down 'em, I'll kick you 'round the camp when I come in." With that he turned from the abashed youngster and went to help Jacko rise. "Sorry, feller, but I had to stop you firing off that gun."

"G-Get your hands off!" Jacko muttered, holding the injured area and shrugging himself away. "I'll——"

"Take your hoss and head back to camp," Red said. "See Rowdy and ask him to give you something for your hurts."

"I—I won't be forgetting——!" Jacko began, then moaned and staggered to one side and vomited. When he had finished, he stumbled to his horse, dragged himself into the saddle and rode awkwardly after the departing Willock.

Red frowned then gave his attention to the girls. Standing up, Dawn went to the waiting *bayo-tigre* and mounted.

"If you pair don't have anything better to do," Red said coldly. "Stay clear of the herd. Get going."

"How dare y——!" Barbe began in a loud voice.

"He's right," Dawn put in. "Turn your hoss and let's get going."

For a moment Barbe glared furiously at the other girl and met cold challenge. Then the dark-haired girl swung her mount and rode after the cowhands. Dawn turned to Red and sighed.

"Damned fool kid!" she said.

"Who me?" asked Red.

"You too. Only I meant that damned fool kid brother of mine. He'd've got licked for sure happen you hadn't cut in."

"And still might, him and Burle both, when Dusty

hears what's come off. You'd best get going back to camp, Dawn. One I'm sorry for's Jacko."

"I reckon he's sorry for his-self," Dawn said without humor. "Only you had to stop him and he's lucky you didn't do it with a gun. We'll not come out here again."

Catching up to Jacko, Dawn tried to show him what might have happened. He only snarled back at her and, wisely, she let the matter drop. Leaving the cowhand, Dawn went after Barbe to catch her just after she joined Willock.

"He had no right to talk to you like that," Barbe was saying when Dawn arrived. "It was shameful and——"

"Yeah!" Willock answered. "I'm not going to forget it."

"You mustn't antagonize him, Burle," Barbe warned. "After all, his uncle is leader of the trail drive."

"Yeah!" Willock muttered. "Goodnight and his kin run the drive."

"Which they don't do bad at it," Dawn commented, deftly inserting her horse between Barbe's and Willock's mounts.

"Depends," Willock grunted.

"What on?" Dawn asked coldly.

"How good friends you are with 'em," the cowhand answered. "There's some of us get on better with 'em than the others do."

"What might that mean?" Dawn demanded.

"Look who's been sent back to the herd," Willock told her.

At that moment they saw Dusty riding toward them. Halting his horse, the small Texan asked Willock what brought him and Jacko away from the herd.

"Maybe you'd best tell him," Willock said to Dawn, a hint of challenge in his voice.

Sucking in an angry breath, Dawn did so. "Sure, if you don't have the guts to," she answered. "Him and Vern got to tangling back there. It was Vern who started the fight——"

"I think that it was no more than a harmless piece of horseplay and neither were to blame," Barbe put in, smiling in her most winning manner at Dusty. Then she put on a frown. "But your cousin had no right to treat them so roughly. He kicked that poor cowboy in the—— Well, he kicked him savagely."

"Jacko tried to pull a gun on Red," Dawn put in and Willock, annoyed at his crony for drawing Barbe's sympathy, nodded agreement.

"Then he got what he asked for and's lucky it's not worse," Dusty said, showing no signs of being won over. "What happened?"

"Red sent me 'n' Jacko back to tell you he wants two more——"

"*Three* more!" Dawn interrupted and corrected Willock. "He said three more. Only reason he didn't send Vern along was he figured you pair'd be *loco* enough to start fussing again on the way in."

"And he'd likely've been right," Dusty said, his voice almost mild. "It sounds like there's not enough work for you knob-heads* out at the herd. I'll have to see if I can't find you something to fill the time."

By that time Willock had come to know Dusty real well and he stifled a groan. One way or another, he figured that he, Jacko and Vern were going to pay a stiff price for their stupid attempts to gain Barbe's favors.

*Knobhead: generally an exceptionally awkward mule.

CHAPTER TWELVE
He's Not Wearing A Gun

Burle Willock found his guess to be correct. Making sure to divide the work evenly, Dusty kept the trio fully occupied. He did so well at it that all of them barely found time to do more than glimpse the source of their rivalry in passing from one chore to the next. At night they found themselves riding guard on the herd or sent to man the lonely picket points Dusty had set out to prevent any chance of a surprise attack. In that manner he kept them away from the camp fire at those times when Barbe was near it. More than that, Dusty had taken each of the trio aside on their return to the camp and given his opinion of their conduct, intelligence and general worth. None had enjoyed the interview. However, Jacko appeared to realize that he had got no more than he deserved and might have been far worse off. The other two promised to mend their ways and seemed to be making a try at doing it. If Barbe felt like going riding again, she never mentioned it.

The work went ahead fast. After a thorough check on each horse in the remuda, a party under Billy Jack started work on replacing missing or badly worn shoes. Under old Boiler Benson's knowing eyes, saddlery was inspected and repairs carried out. Then the cook organized the unloading of the chuck and bed wagons, bracing each of them in its turn so that its wheels could be removed and the axles greased. On the morning of the fourth day only the de Martins' wagon remained to be put in a condition where it could survive the hazardous crossing.

Wanting to see if they had learned their lesson, Dusty let Vern, Willock and Jacko help the photographer empty the wagon. Having Mark in charge, he felt that any trouble would be dealt with promptly. Although Vern and Willock scowled at and studiously pretended to ignore each other, they gave every appearance of having profited by the lessons of the past days.

Boxes and trunks came from the wagon, while Barbe hovered around. One of the boxes gave off a familiar clinking sound which drew interested looks from Willock and Jacko.

"Thirsty work this, Jacko," Willock commented, flickering a gaze at Barbe as they spoke.

"Sure is," Jacko agreed, running his tongue tip over his lips. "And nothing but water to take for it."

"You have nothing but water?" Barbe asked.

"Nary a thing but that 'n' coffee," Willock agreed. "Colonel Charlie don't allow no hard liquor on his drive."

At that moment Mark came into sight around the end of the wagon and the conversation ended. The work went on without incident and toward evening they started to reload the wagon. While passing a box up to where Turkey stood at the tailgate, Vern heard the sound of approaching hooves. Both of them turned to look, each expecting the other to retain his hold. Instead neither did, so the box fell and burst open. It held items of feminine underclothing and a large, leather-bound book. The latter bounced and landed open at the feet of de Martin and Dusty as they walked toward Goodnight's returning party.

"You clumsy b——" Barbe began furiously, then chopped off her words as de Martin glared at her.

Bending down to help gather the scattered contents, Dusty found himself looking at several photographs in the book. All appeared to be of a wedding and in one de Martin stood at Barbe's side. He wore a top hat and fashionable suit while she was dressed in white, with a veil over her hair and bouquet of flowers in her hands. Before Dusty could do more than glimpse the picture, Barbe snatched the book from him and slammed it shut.

"I'll take that!" she said, going to place it in the box.

"I'm sorry, Dusty," de Martin said. "But there are a few photographs which Barbe regards as embarrassing. That was a picture of our cousin's wedding. Barbe was maid-of-honor and I was best man. It *was* disappointing. The rumor that the best man has the first night just isn't true."

"I found that out for myself," Dusty admitted, watching a spluttering Vern and Turkey blushingly help Barbe pick up the remainder of the contents. They hurriedly handed over the various garments and she packed the box then let them place it in the wagon. "I'd best go and see what Uncle Charlie found out."

"May I come with you?" de Martin asked.

"Feel free," Dusty replied and called some of the men to give orders that they should take care of the new arrivals' horses. "How'd it go, Uncle Charlie?"

"No worse than we expected," Goodnight replied. "There's been some rain up this way, but we'll still have three days of solid dry driving to reach the Pecos. We'll start the crossing at sun-up tomorrow."

"May I offer a suggestion, Charles?" de Martin put in.

"Go to it."

"If Dusty doesn't have any further plans for us, how about letting all hands have a night's relaxation?"

"How do you mean?"

"I understand that Rowdy plays the fiddle and has one along. Perhaps we could have a social evening. Of course Barbe and Dawn won't be able to partner the whole crew for dancing——"

"That's easy enough settled," Dusty smiled. "We'll put a heifer-brand on some of the boys."

"I don't follow you," de Martin said.

"It's the way we have out here, usually being short on women for dances and such," Goodnight explained. "So some of the fellers have a white rag tied around their left arms and dance 'lady' fashion."

"Not many of them object to being heifer-branded, seeing's how they get to sit with the ladies," Dusty went on. "Although they most times wind up looking at the bar most unladylike."

"That won't happen tonight," Goodnight stated. "They can fun all they like, but there'll be no drinking."

"With Rowdy keeping his medicine bottle locked up tight in the wagon, they won't have anything to drink," Dusty replied. "I'll fix things up, if it's all right with you, Uncle Charlie."

"Go to it," the rancher authorized. "Ask Miss Barbe and Dawn to lend you a hand while you're at it."

News of the proposed evening's entertainment was greeted with considerable enthusiasm by the trail crew. Dusty warned them that night herding would continue, but agreed to leave off the pickets. Knowing that the cattle came first, the cowhands raised no objections. Especially when they discovered that he had organized a rota which allowed everybody to spend as much time as possible at the festivities.

Due to the shortage of "for real" lady partners—heifer brands formed a poor substitute—Dawn was excused taking her turn on the night herd. Following the rangeland custom, she and Barbe were permitted to select the men who wore the heifer brands. Although Dusty did not care for the girls picking Vern and Willock, they produced a mighty good argument in favor of their choice. That way neither cowhand could partner Barbe, removing a cause of friction between them. So Dusty gave in, it being the ladies' prerogative to select their own company.

Certainly the dance began with reasonable decorum, Barbe wore the dress in which she had presented herself on the night she arrived and Dawn produced a gingham frock brought along to use on reaching Fort Sumner. The music was supplied by Rowdy on his battered violin, Turkey playing a jew's harp and Swede Ahlén giving backing with a blow-fiddle.* Perhaps the sounds they emitted would not have been acceptable in a fancy Eastern hotel, but the uncritical audience buckled down to dancing with vim if not grace.

After a few dances, somebody called on the Kid for a song. Once he had obliged with such of Juan Ortega's story as was fit for mixed company, other members of the crew responded with their party-pieces. Everything was going smoothly and in such good spirits that Dusty relaxed. It seemed that Vern and Willock had forgotten the fight. Certainly they made the most of their "heifer-brand" positions, by allowing their "partners" to bring them cups of coffee or the minor luxuries Rowdy had been able to produce at such short notice for the "guests." Even Heenan appeared to be joining in the fun for Dusty saw him handing a cup of coffee to Willock in an interval between the dance sets.

"And I tell you there ain't nobody can lick Swede Ahlén at Injun wrestling!" Solly Sodak of the Lazy F announced in a loud voice during a lull in the noise and brought every eye his way.

"Mark there can," objected Red Blaze, having been involved with the cowhand in a discussion for some minutes. "Which I've got five whole dollars to prove it."

"How about that Swede," called Sodak. "Are you going to help me get rich at ole Red's expense?"

Once brought up, the subject aroused much interest and demanded settlement. Never averse to putting his skill and strength on display, Ahlén suggested that he and Mark should satisfy the bettors promptly.

Producing his sturdy chopping block and muttering dire warnings of what would happen if it be damaged in any way, Rowdy set it in position by the fire. Taking up

---

*Blow-fiddle: An empty whiskey jug used as a kind of wind instrument.

their places on either side of the block, each of the contestants rested his right elbow on the chopping surface and gripped the other's raised right hand. Appointed judge, Rowdy waited until the audience had formed around the block and gave the order to start.

"I've got ten dollars's says it lasts for more than twenty minutes," a man said and another took the bet.

Certainly all knew that they faced a lengthy session of Indian wrestling, for the contestants were evenly matched. Mark's slight advantage in strength was counterbalanced by Ahlén's extra experience. Excitement filled the audience as the seconds ticked away and they were oblivious of anything but the two men at the chopping block. Straining in their efforts to force down the opposing hand, Mark and Ahlén put all their considerable strength into beating the other.

Shortly after the contest began, Willock became aware that Barbe was not in the crowd. Looking around, he saw her going toward the de Martins' wagon and edged back to follow her.

Laughter, advice—mostly impractical or impossible—and offers of further bets flashed noisily among the spectators. So great was the racket that it drowned out the sounds of cursing, shouting and scuffling from behind the de Martin wagon. Dusty was first to become aware of the trouble, although up to that point he had not noticed certain absentees from the crowd.

Suddenly Willock reeled into sight from behind the wagon. Catching his balance, he drove out a blow at the head of Vern as the youngster followed him. Running into Willock's fist, Vern went backwards and sat down hard.

"Don't shoot him!" Barbe screamed, appearing beyond the two cowhands.

Spitting out a curse and mouthful of blood, Vern stabbed his hand toward his side. Already moving in to attack, Willock skidded to a halt, drew and fired. Vern rocked backward as lead ripped into his chest and sprawled on to the ground.

Dusty went through the crowd as if it did not exist. At the sound of the shot, Mark and Ahlén released each other. The rest of the crowd forgot the contest, bets, everything except what met their eyes as they faced the de Martins' wagon. A concerted rush followed on the small Texan's heels. Faster than the rest, Dawn reached her brother almost as soon as Dusty. She went to her knees at Vern's side, staring at the wound and reading its serious nature.

Tense and watchful, yet without making a hostile movement, Dusty faced Willock. Every sense the small Texan possessed warned him of danger. After shooting the youngster, Willock had recocked his revolver. Now he stood on spread-apart legs, with an over-casually balanced stance that, taken with the loose-lipped, slobbering grin on his face, screamed a deadly warning to one experienced in such signs. For all that, Dusty could not believe Willock was drunk no matter how he looked or acted. Silence fell on the crowd behind Dusty as they waited for him to make a move.

"What happened?" Dusty asked quietly.

"The fodder-forker pushed his luck too far is what," Willock replied, his voice slightly slurred but tuned to sound tough and mean.

"Vern's dead!" Dawn gasped, looking at the two men.

"So he was going for his gun and I stopped him!" Willock growled. "That's——"

"He's not wearing a gun!" Red Blaze put in, having moved forward to kneel at Dawn's side. "His holster's empty."

Angry comments rumbled up at the words. Looking over his shoulder, Dusty saw Narth moving forward with the Swinging G cowhands flanking him. At the same time, Jacko and two other Mineral Wells men came together. Dusty was suddenly aware that all but Ahlén of the older Mineral Wells men were riding the night herd. That deprived him of what might have been a restraining influence. Dusty's sense of danger increased. There was trouble in the air, a peril to the success of the herd as serious as any Hayden's hired guns might have caused. One wrong word or move might easily explode the whole camp into blazing gunplay.

"If that's right——!" Narth began grimly.

"I'll handle it," Goodnight interrupted, joining Dusty. "Put the gun up, Burle, and let's talk this out."

"What's to talk about?" the cowhand demanded truculently. "I pulled on him when Miss Barbe yelled. How was I to know he didn't have a gun?"

"Easily enough," de Martin commented, walking to his sister's side from the rear of the wagon. "You'd seen Vern loan me his gun so that I didn't go unarmed into the bushes."

"Why you——" Narth spat out, right hand, dropping to his Colt's butt.

Fingers like steel grasped Narth's fist, crushing it in a powerful grip and preventing him from drawing the gun. Twisting his head, the cowhand looked into Mark Counter's face and heard the other's soft-spoken warning.

"Leave it be, *amigo*. Colonel Charlie'll see the right's done."

Slowly Dawn raised her head. No tears came, but her face held lines of grief and anger. Lifting her eyes to Goodnight's she said in a bitter voice, "What're you going to do about it, Colonel? He murdered my brother."

Again the low rumble of comment rose. Every man in the camp knew of the last grim article in the contract they had signed before leaving the Swinging G. Looking back, Dusty saw two separate groups starting to form. About half of the men, Goodnight's hands included, moved to where Narth stood by Mark. The second party consisted of Willock's cronies and looked to Ahlén for guidance. As the accused cowhand's segundo, Jacko and the others wanted to know where the big blond stood in the affair.

So did Dusty, come to that, and he asked, "How about it, Swede?"

"We can take him——" Austin began.

"Open your mouth again!" Dusty blazed, swinging toward the speaker. "And I'll close it with my boot—— Mark, take Austin, Spat and Eddie to the night herd. Eph, Ross, go help Will Trinka on the remuda."

"Get to it!" Goodnight went on, knowing what Dusty wanted to do.

Slowly, showing their reluctance, the Swinging G men turned to obey. Usually Eph Horn and Ross Phares would not be sent to assist the night hawk with the horses but Dusty wanted to give Ahlén proof that he would deal fairly with Willock and not rely on the hands loyal to Goodnight to enforce his demands.

Swiftly Dusty looked around. Kneeling at her brother's side, Dawn was silent. It seemed that she had realized what her words might cause, for she never took her eyes from Goodnight's face although she said no more. From her, Dusty turned his attention to the de Martins. They and Heenan once more stood clear of the two factions. Considering what had happened, Barbe seemed remarkably calm. She watched the scene before her with an almost detached interest.

Diverting his thoughts from the girls, Dusty studied the trail hands. His dismissal of the Swinging G men had lessened the tension slightly. Yet everything depended on how Swede Ahlén answered Dusty's question. If he stood by the Articles of Agreement, Willock's supporters would go along. If not, the small Texan did not care to think of the result. Swede Ahlén held several lives and the safety of the whole trail drive in his big hands. Should he go back on his word about the contract, Josh Narth would want to dispense his own justice. While Willock's cronies might stand for Goodnight or Dusty dealing with the situation, they certainly would not permit another trail hand to do so.

After what seemed an age, although it followed on the heels of Dusty giving his orders to Mark, Ahlén spoke.

"Put up the gun, Burle. We're going to hold a hearing on the killing."

"The hell you are!" Willock spat back, making no attempt to comply. What chance do I have? You've seen how all that bunch stand together."

Ahlén stiffened slightly, looking at the cowhand's face and moving to stand between Dusty and Goodnight. "He's liquored up. Watch him. He's dangerous when he's wet."

Hearing the words, Dusty and Goodnight let out low

breaths of annoyance. Under the Articles of Agreement, no liquor could be carried by the trail hands. Yet Willock showed every sign of being drunk and, according to his foreman, was a bad *hombre* when in that condition. Which altered nothing in the basic issue. It only made the situation more dangerously explosive.

"All ri——" Goodnight began, making as if to step forward.

"Keep back, all of you!" Willock snarled, his Colt making an arc that took in the three men before him. "I'm full to my guts with this drive and I'm quitting. Who's coming with me?"

"Nobody," Goodnight said quietly. "And you're not going either."

"Who'll stop me?" snarled Willock.

"I will," Goodnight answered.

"No, Uncle Charlie," Dusty put in gently. "The segundo handles the men. I let this start, so it's for me to see it through."

There was another, unmentioned point. Without its trail boss, the herd could not get through. So Dusty figured if anybody was going to be shot, he could be better spared than his uncle.

"I'll kill the first to move!" Willock snarled.

"Then you'll have to do it," Dusty replied and took a step forward.

"You'll have to drop us both," Ahlén warned, advancing in line with Dusty. "Don't be *loco*, Burle. Leather it. You know Colonel Charlie'll give you a fair hearing."

Backing off before the steady advance of the two men, Willock looked from one to the other. Drunk he might be, but not sufficiently for his condition to have driven all sense and thought from his head. Swede Ahlén had never professed to be a gunfighter, but possessed the gritty determination to push through anything he started. Yet, more menacing to Willock at that moment was the *big* blond man ranged at his segundo's side. A quick glance warned Willock that he could not expect help from his cronies. Even Jacko stood silent and clearly willing to accept Ahlén's assurance that justice would be done.

Sweat ran down Willock's face and indecision played on it. Watching him, Dusty knew that he might go either way. If he should be drunk, impossible as it seemed, he could either surrender or make a rat-like fight against what he regarded as a trap.

For each pace the two men advanced, Willock retreated a stride. To Dusty it seemed that the barrel of the cowhand's Colt started to dip. At that moment a shot rang out. Lead ripped into Willock's head, spinning him around and tumbling him lifeless almost at the small Texan's feet.

Smoke curled up from the revolver in Heenan's hand and he said, "I thought he was fixing to start throwing lead."

CHAPTER THIRTEEN

Where Did You Hire Heenan?

Throwing a look at the Mineral Wells men, Dusty prepared to draw if they showed signs of hostility. None of them made a move, but stood staring at the still body at the small Texan's feet.

"You stupid son-of-a-bitch!" Ahlén growled at Heenan. "He was giving it up."

"It didn't look that way to me!" the hardcase answered, holstering his gun. "Hell! If he'd thrown lead, this whole camp'd've gone up smoking. And if he'd run, we were standing in his way."

On the face of it, Heenan had acted in a sensible manner. The moment Willock squeezed his trigger, the rest of the men would have become involved. That would place the innocent bystanders in considerable danger. Nor would their position have been any safer if Willock had elected to escape, for they stood in his path to freedom.

"You can hardly blame Mr. Heenan, Swede," de Martin put in. "I thought that Burle meant to shoot you."

"Best get two graves dug," Dusty said quietly. "Lon, take after Mark, then go on to Billy Jack and tell them everything's all right here."

"Yo!" replied the Kid, whistling for his stallion and darting into the darkness to meet it.

Slowly Dawn rose and turned her grief-lined face toward Dusty. It was not her first brush with violent death, or even the first time she had lost somebody close to her, so she held control of her emotions and showed no sign of breaking down. That might come later. Right then she had other things on her mind. From Dusty she turned to Barbe, eyeing the girl with cold mistrust.

"How did it start?" Dawn demanded.

"They—they followed me," Barbe replied hesitantly. "I had come to the wagon to help Edmond collect his camera so that we might photograph the fun. I thought that they wanted to help——"

"So did I," de Martin went on. "When I said I wanted to go into the bushes, Vern loaned me his Colt——"

"Who started the fight?" Jacko interrupted.

"Finding out now won't do anybody any good," Dusty put in. "Burle Willock'd been drinking. Where'd he get the liquor?"

"Could he have had it with him all the time?" asked de Martin. "Waiting for a chance to celebrate, I mean."

"Not him," Ahlén grunted. "He wasn't a booze-hound, but he liked it enough to have drunk any he'd brought long afore tonight."

"None of the others in the crew had any either," Dusty said. "Except Rowdy. Go see if your stock's still there, Rowdy."

"Sure, Cap'n," answered the cook and went to obey. On his return, he held out a partially filled bottle of whiskey. "That's what there was left in it after I yanked a tooth out for Sherm Sherman."

"Which leaves you, Edmond," Dusty drawled.

"How dare you imply that my brot——!" Barbe started hotly.

"Dusty is right, dear," de Martin cut in. "I do have liquor in my wagon and this is a serious matter which needs clearing up. You can inspect my stock, Dusty. I have kept it under lock and key since Charles explained his no-drinking article."

With that the photographer led the way to his wagon and insisted that an inspection be made of his liquor supply. As he had claimed, it was securely locked in a trunk to which he carried the only key. Leaving the wagon, Dusty remembered something he had seen earlier and turned to Heenan.

"You took Burle a cup of coffee——"

"Sure," agreed the hardcase. "Two of 'em. Hell, it was all part of the running, us treating the heifer—brands like they was for-real womenfolk."

"Mr. Heenan has no liquor with him, Dusty," de Martin stated. "He was broke when he came to work for me and I refused to advance his wages to buy a bottle."

"It—it's all my fault!" Barbe put in, sniffing and looking pathetically at the men. "You all blame me——"

"No, ma'am!" Jacko hastened to assure her. "We ain't none of us blaming you."

"Those boys've been fussing over you——" Dawn began.

"And I did my best to stay away from them after that fight!" Barbe whimpered. "You all know that. I never went near either of them. And tonight it was I who suggested that they played at being women so that I wouldn't have to dance with either of them. You all know that."

"We all saw it," Sodak agreed. "Ain't nobody blaming you, Miss Barbe."

"There for sure ain't!" Jackie confirmed, directing a grim, challenging look around him.

Barbe threw the young cowhand a look of abject relief and complete gratitude. Then she clasped her handkerchief to her face, turned and ran to her wagon. Sobs shook at her as she climbed inside.

"You'd best see to her, Edmond." Goodnight said. "Rowdy, take some of the crew and have two graves dug. We'll have to bury—Vern—tonight, Dawn."

"I—I know!" Dawn replied. "Oh Colonel Charlie, he was only a boy——"

Showing a gentleness known by only his closest friends, Goodnight took the girl in his arms and led her away from the bodies. Quietly Rowdy assembled a working party and, for once, none of the cowhands objected to riding the blister-end of a shovel. Watching them go, Dusty let out an angry growl which brought Ahlén's eyes to him.

"Damn it, Swede!" Dusty said. "Where did he get that liquor?"

"I wish I knew," the big cowhand answered. "Whoever gave it to him near on blew this whole drive into the air."

Red-eyed from crying, stiff-faced and tight-lipped, Dawn took her regular place among a silent trail crew on the morning after the double killing. She had seen her brother buried the night before and sobbed almost to sunup in the bedwagon, but insisted at breakfast that she was able to take her share of the workload. If anything, her brother's death had increased her determination to see the drive brought off successfully.

"Ho, cattle!" Mark and Ahlén chanted at the point. "Ho! Ho! Ho! Ho!"

Showing satisfaction almost, Buffalo lurched into motion. There was a short period of inevitable confusion until the steers reassumed their positions in the line. Wending their way to the banks of the South Concho, the cattle drank and crossed without any trouble to resume their westward march on the other side.

"We've not lost more than half-a-dozen head," Dusty told his uncle as they gathered to compare their totals after making a trail count on the western side of the river.

"You've done well, boy," Goodnight congratulated.

"Not all that well," Dusty said bitterly, thinking of the two graves close to their deserted campsite.

"Very well!" Goodnight insisted. "Including last night. A wrong word or move there would have seen more graves on the Horsehead Crossing."

Early in their stay, one of the hands had found a horse's

skull near the river and stuck it up in a tree to give the area a name it would bear in future.

"Swede did most of it," Dusty said. "If he'd not backed us, there'd've been powder burned last night."

"Swede's got a good head on his shoulders, like you. That's why I stayed out of it and let you two call the play. I'm damned if I know what I'll say to Darby Sutherland when we get back home."

"I know how you feel, sir. That was one chore I hated in the War; and I only had to write letters, not tell them face to face. It'd be best if we watched the crew real careful for a few days, Uncle Charlie, and try to make sure that nothing else happens to stir them up."

"It would," Goodnight agreed. "Once we get on to the Staked Plains, they'll have more then plenty to keep them occupied."

"Sure. I wonder where Willock got the liquor from?"

"He could've carried it all along. After being off it for so long, he'd not need much to make him drunk."

"I asked Miss de Martin why she shouted about not shooting," Dusty said. "She reckons she can't remember doing it. I didn't push it, she likely feels bad enough about what's happened."

During the day, Dusty kept a close watch on the crew. They were subdued in their manner, but worked together with no sign of remembering the split of the previous night. So far they had not got on to the real Staked Plains, but the grazing grew poorer while the heat increased. By good fortune they found a water hole and let the cattle drink before bedding down for the night.

Despite Dusty's comments, Barbe seemed to have recovered from her shock by nightfall. Returning from a visit to the remuda, Dusty heard talking beyond a clump of bushes. Recognizing Barbe's voice, he would have walked on but her companion's words brought him to a halt.

"Colonel Charlie won't let me do it," said Austin Hoffman. "He wouldn't let Edmond take pictures close to the cattle."

"But you could do it, Austin," Barbe answered. "And it

would make both my brother and I so grateful if you did."

"They'd not let me do it either," Austin protested.

"Couldn't you do it without them knowing?"

"How?"

"Take the camera and hide close by. Then photograph the herd as it comes toward you."

"That'd mean being on foot," Austin gasped.

"Are you afraid?" Barbe asked and Dusty could sense her bristling at the arguments.

"No. But I'm not *loco* neither," Austin replied. "Any one of them critters'd charge me on sight——"

"It would be worth the risk, Austin," Barbe purred. "Just think what such a photograph would mean. The first of its kind, taken at considerable risk. Why it would make you famous. Then, with the flair you show for photography, you could open a studio in Austin, or even in some Eastern city where I could live. Don't you see, Austin?"

At which point Dusty decided to let his presence be known. So he gave a rasping cough and heard a hurried scuffling among the bushes.

"Who's there?" Dusty called.

"It's only us," Austin answered, coming through the undergrowth with the girl trailing behind him. "We're just going back to camp."

"I'll come with you," Dusty said. "Hey, I just now remembered, Austin. There was a Hoffman in the Texas Light, maybe you're kin to him?"

"My uncle," Hoffman confirmed, looking just a touch relieved and showing no sign of yielding to Barbe's glances at the bushes. "What do you know, Miss Barbe, Cap'n Dusty knowed my uncle in the War."

"How interesting!" Barbe said in a tone which carried a knife's edge.

"Say, Miss Barbe," Dusty drawled. "You don't know if Edmond's figuring to take any pictures of the herd in the next few days?"

"He may be," Barbe answered, darting a suspicious glance at the small Texan and reading nothing on his face.

"I'd best ask him not to," Dusty said. "Especially close

up. That powder going off near them might start a stampede and none of us'd want that to happen—now would we, Austin?"

"We sure's hell wouldn't," Hoffman agreed vehemently.

"I'm sure pleased that I met up with you, Miss Barbe," Dusty went on in a matter-of-fact tone. "It'll save me looking up your brother special to warn him. You can do it for me."

"I will," Barbe promised, but her voice dripped ice and she left the men as soon as they drew near to the camp.

"How much did you hear, Cap'n Dusty?" Austin asked as soon as they were alone. "Afore you coughed, I mean."

"Enough to figure it was my business to cough," Dusty replied. "Don't try it, Austin. Even if you don't get killed by a steer, you'll stampede the herd. Either way, you'll never get that fancy photographic studio in some Eastern town."

After the cowhand had left him, Dusty stood for a moment and looked at the de Martin wagon. However, he put off his intention to see the photographer with a warning not to use Barbe as a lure to get risky pictures taken. There would be time to do that later. So Dusty walked across to the main fire and heard Goodnight talking to the crew. One of the hands had just been complaining about his bed being so rock-studded that he doubted if he could sleep.

"Getting to sleep's not going to worry you for a spell after tonight, anyways," the rancher announced.

"How come, Colonel Charlie?" the cowhand inquired.

"Because when we move out tomorrow," Goodnight explained and something in his voice brought all other conversation to a halt, "we won't be stopping until we reach the Pecos."

An almost numbed silence followed the words, as the trail crew gave thought to the implication behind them. Even the de Martin party had heard, for they approached the fire. Dawn could see concern on the girl's face and wondered what caused it.

"You mean that we just keep the herd going," Ahlén

said. "Without bedding down, or for water, until we get to the other side, Colonel?"

"That's just what I mean," the rancher agreed. "You saw the lie of the land, Swede. There'll barely be enough water for the horses and crew. So we keep the cattle going for as long as it takes us to hit the Pecos."

"How about food for the hands?" Sherman wanted to know.

"Rowdy'll pull ahead with the wagon, throw up a meal and you'll eat it in the saddle. Those cattle have to be kept moving all the time."

"How about my sister, Charles?" asked de Martin. "Do you expect her to be subjected to such conditions?"

"There's no other choice," Goodnight answered.

"What you could do," Dusty suggested, "is stop back at night, then catch up during the day. Your wagon'll be able to make better time than we can with the herd."

"Would that be safe?" de Martin inquired.

"Safe enough," Dusty replied. "There're no Indians up this way and we'll be leaving a trail a blind man could follow. If there should be a sandstorm, I'll get Lon back to guide you."

"We'll see how it goes first," the photographer decided, taking Barbe's arm as she opened her mouth. "Come, dear. I think we had better get a good night's sleep, don't you?"

"If you say so," Barbe answered, her voice brittle.

"Edmond's got a right smart idea," Dusty remarked as the couple walked away. "We're all going to need our sleep with what's ahead. I don't know about the rest of you, but I'm riding herd on my blankets right now."

The feeling appeared to be generally accepted and soon the camp had settled itself down for what would be their last night's sleep until they reached the Pecos.

Always a light sleeper, and never more so than when acting as a scout, the Kid woke as some slight, alien noise reached his ears. The normal camp sounds had left him undisturbed. Neither the changing of the night guard nor one of the crew leaving the camp to relieve himself had woken the dark youngster. Yet faint footsteps brought him from his sleep. Apart from a casual-appearing roll over in his blankets, he gave no sign of the change in his condition. Looking around, he saw nothing apparently changed. The crew still slept around the fire, except for the empty beds of the night herders. Yet somebody had sneaked away from the camp, of that he felt certain.

In a swift, silent movement, the Kid quit his blankets and rose. He wore moccasins, was bareheaded, fully-dressed and held his bowie knife. Glancing at the rifle and Dragoon Colt on his bed, he decided they would not be needed. So he flitted into the darkness without disturbing the other sleepers.

Whoever had woken the Kid was going toward the bedded-down herd a quarter of a mile from the camp. On fast-striding, noiseless feet, the Kid followed. At last he saw a crouching figure moving through the darkness. Not fifty yards from the nearest of the steers, the figure halted. Something metallic glinted in its hand and the rapidly approaching Kid knew what it was.

"Drop it!" hissed the Kid.

"What the——?" snarled a familiar voice and the figure spun around, right arm bending to point at the dark youngster.

Knowing what the other had planned to do, the Kid did not hesitate. Up then down swung his right hand. Leaving it, the bowie knife flashed through the air. Such was the weight, balance and cutting edge of the great knife, powered by the Kid's trained right arm, that it severed a way through the snooper's ribs and sank its clip point into the vital organs they protected. Reeling, the night-sneaker let his revolver drop unfired. Vainly his hands tried to draw out the knife during the brief time he had to live. Buckling at the knees, his legs deposited him face down on the ground.

"Who-all's that?" called a voice and Mark Counter rode from the darkness.

"You had a caller," the Kid replied, rolling over his victim and retrieving the knife. "Likely Dusty'll be interested to know who it is."

Which statement proved correct. On his return, the

Kid found the cook and louse already preparing breakfast. Going to Dusty, the Kid shook him gently until he woke. Hearing what his dark *amigo* had to tell, Dusty rose immediately.

"Let's go and see what de Martin's got to say," Dusty growled.

"His bed's not under the wagon," the Kid said as they walked that way. "I missed seeing that."

"Where the hell is he then?" Dusty asked.

De Martin supplied the answer by looking from the rear of the wagon's canopy. With ruffled hair and his torso bare, he gave signs of having been recently woken. Yet he had always bedded down under the wagon, except during the rainy period.

"What's wrong?" the photographer asked.

"Can you come out here, Edmond?" Dusty said.

"Of course. Just a moment," de Martin agreed and ducked back out of sight. The Texans heard him talking with his sister, then he appeared wearing a bathrobe which had been much admired by the cowhands on previous occasions. "What is it?"

"Heenan," drawled the Kid.

"What about him?" asked the photographer.

"I just now killed him for trying to stompede the herd."

There was no doubt that the words came as a shock to de Martin. Nor had the Kid done anything to lessen their impact, wanting to see how the other reacted.

"I—I don't understand!" de Martin gasped.

"Nor do we," Dusty assured him. "Where did you hire Heenan?"

"In Graham. It was soon after we learned that Charles had already left with his herd. Heenan came to me and offered to act as my guide. From what he said, I formed the opinion he wished to leave Texas to avoid a feud. As he asked a reasonable wage, I agreed."

"You took a big chance, hiring a stranger like that," the Kid remarked.

"It seemed safe enough," the photographer answered. "I knew that we would soon catch up with the herd. Please, Dusty. Can we continue this later? My sister was so disturbed at the thought of crossing the Staked Plains that I spent the night in the wagon to calm her. I wouldn't want her made more nervous."

"I reckon we can," Dusty decided. "Let's go, Lon."

"What do you reckon, Dusty?" the Kid inquired as they walked away.

"If Heenan was working for Hayden, coming with Edmond and his sister'd be a good way to get accepted by us," Dusty replied. "Then he waited his chance, or for help to catch up. When it didn't come, he figured to scatter the herd. After the trouble at Horsehead Crossing, the crew'd not be too eager to gather the steers and go on."

"Even if they did, it'd slow us down so we'd not get to Fort Sumner on time," the Kid went on. "I'll bet on one thing, though. De Martin didn't know what Heenan planned."

"That's for sure," Dusty agreed. "Nobody could act as surprised as he looked. Come on, we'd best go tell Uncle Charlie what's happened."

CHAPTER FOURTEEN

If This Keeps Up, I'll Go Mad

When told of Heenan's attempt at stampeding the herd and death, Goodnight agreed with Dusty's views about the former. However, the urgent nature of the drive's next phase soon pushed all thoughts of the incident from his and Dusty's heads. To avoid complications, they passed the word that Heenan had deserted during the night. Filled with the knowledge of what lay ahead, the trail hands accepted the excuse and were not greatly interested in why the hardcase had gone.

When the cattle started moving that morning, there began an epic journey in the history of the West. For years to come, the first crossing of the Staked Plains by a trail herd would be spoken of with awe. Certainly the people involved would never forget it. Just as Goodnight had warned, they kept going without a pause by day or night.

At the point, Boiler Benson and Billy Jack took over the usual leaders. The giant strength of Mark and Ahlén was of more use with the drag. There they and other men tailed up steers which had fallen or just lay down to quit, or pushed aside the stronger steers to ease the path for the weaker. Masked by bandanas to try to keep the churned-up dust from clogging their nostrils and mouths, the remainder of the crew found work in plenty. Heat-crazed steers fought among themselves or showed the savage aggression of stick-teased rattlesnakes. More than one of the trail hands owed his life to the speed and sure-footedness of his horse, when attacked by a raging longhorn. Snatching meals in the saddle, dismounting only when nature could no longer be resisted, they rode on and on, ever west.

Ranging far ahead of the others, dependent upon his *Pehnane* upbringing and the ability of his horses, the Kid sought out the deadly alkali or salt lakes. Once located, he checked on the wind's direction and passed the word to Goodnight who changed the line of march to pass so that the smell of water was not carried to the cattle. In that way they avoided the greatest danger of all. Fights could be stopped, charges evaded, the weary kept moving or the "downers" hauled up and made to walk. Let the thirsty cattle get but one sniff of the water and they would have pushed to it with a force that no man nor horse could hope to halt.

Through the three days of the drive, Dawn took her share of the work, risks and hardships. In fact, the way she plunged herself into the thickest, hardest of the grueling toil, it seemed that she sought to fill both her own and her dead brother's places. Not only did she work hard, but her presence acted as the spur Dusty had hoped it would. What cowhand would quit, no matter how tired or dispirited he might be, when he saw the girl carrying on? At times Dawn being on hand prevented an exhausted cowboy from just giving up. Although every muscle, fiber and bone ached with weariness, the girl continued to ride the herd.

On the morning of the fourth—and they hoped last—day, Dusty sent Dawn back to see if the de Martins were all right. His main reason for the order was to take the girl from the dangers of the herd, if only for a short time. Reluctantly she agreed and rode away through the dust of the drag.

Even the girl did not realize just how tired she was. Once clear of the constant exertion and the ever-present need to remain alert, she found trouble in keeping her eyes open. In fact she actually went to sleep, only her years of riding training keeping her balanced in the saddle. The sound of a female voice raised in anger jolted Dawn awake. Staring ahead, she found that her *bayo-tigre* gelding was approaching her destination. The de Martins' wagon stood with its team unhitched and flaps opened so that the approaching girl could see inside. Dressed in a robe, a disheveled Barbe faced de Martin furiously.

"If this keeps up, I'll go mad!" the black-haired girl was screaming. "You said it would all be over before we had to——"

At that moment the photographer slapped his sister hard across the cheek. The force of the blow knocked her sprawling on to the unmade bed, sobbing in pain. Then he heard the sound of Dawn's horse. Whirling around, he snatched a Remington Double Derringer from the top of a trunk to line it in the newcomer's direction.

"Oh it's you, Dawn!" de Martin greeted, lowering the little hideout pistol.

"Cap'n Dusty sent me back to see if everything's all right," Dawn replied, wondering where a dude like the photographer had learned such fast, efficient gun handling.

A muffled croak broke from the weeping Barbe, but de Martin went to her side and laid a hand on her shoulder. "It is," he assured Dawn. "My sister was just a little hysterical and I had to quieten her, but we're all right."

"Will she be all right?"

"Yes. I can take care of her."

"Can I help you hitch up your team, or anything?"

"No!" de Martin stated emphatically. "You've probably got enough on your hands with the herd."

"That's for sure," Dawn admitted. "Well, if there's nothing I can do——"

"Not a thing," de Martin insisted. "In fact, I can probably cope with Barbe better alone——"

"Sure," Dawn said. "You'll find the chuck wagon maybe a mile and a half along the trail. I'll get back to the herd."

With that, she rode in the direction of the herd. Curiosity made her turn in the saddle when about a hundred yards from the wagon. De Martin was bending over his sister talking in what Dawn felt to be an angry manner. Figuring it was none of her business, the girl continued to ride after the herd. Before she had reached the drag, something happened to make her put the de Martins out of her mind.

Up at the point, Billy Jack and Boiler Benson saw Buffalo start to sniff the air in a restless manner. At a signal from the oldtimer, Goodnight and Dusty rode up. They too noticed the change in the lead steer's behavior and turned worried faces to each other.

"There's a lake among the broken country ahead!" Dusty said worriedly. "If the wind's changed——"

"Yes!" Goodnight answered and the one word was encyclopedic in its inference.

More of the leading steers raised their heads, joining Buffalo in excited bawling. The sounds rose to a crescendo as the legweary longhorns increased their pace. From a weary, dragging gait, they changed to a hesitant trot, then to a faster run. Soon the front section of the herd was racing forward with a dogged, blind determination that knew no stopping.

"God damn all fool —— —— —— steers!" Goodnight cursed impotently and profanely as the tired cowhands tried to halt the rush.

A mile fell behind, then two, with no sign of the cause for the steers' behavior. At last Billy Jack saw the sun glinting on something ahead. For all his previous gloomy predictions, the cowhand felt a sickening sense of frustration and rage. After so long they were in danger of losing most of the herd. Unless——

"It's not a lake!" Billy Jack screamed the words above

the sounds of hooves, bellowing steers and shouting men. "By the Good Lord, it's the Pecos!"

"It's the Pecos!" Catching the words, another of the hands sent them ringing through the air. "It's the lovely, son-of-a-bitching Pecos!"

So it was. Instead of a lake with misery and death in every mouthful, the water ahead was the Pecos River. Scented almost three miles back by the steers, it had drawn them on and given the inducement they needed to reach it.

By that time the herd had spread itself into a long, segmented line as the fitter steers drew ahead. Even the drags had caught the fever of excitement and were pushing along at their best possible speed, although Mark and his eight-strong party still found the need to help the weakest.

Down to the river's bank rushed the leading cattle. Buffalo and the first of the steers plunged in without hesitation, only to be pushed through by the crush from behind. Yet even that was not as dangerous as it might have been, for they went on, turning back and moving up or downstream until they found a place to enter and drink.

Among the cowhands accompanying the front of the herd, Dawn followed the cattle toward the Pecos. Knowing her strength limited her usefulness in the drag, she had pushed on along the line to help try to stop the rush. Keeping with men, she rode into the river. Profane hilarity filled the air as rider after rider flung himself from his saddle to disappear beneath the surface. Coming up, gasping and spluttering, Dawn looked around her. While the Pecos River lacked the sparkling, crystal-clear quality of a snow-fed mountain brook, none of the crew thought the less of it. At that moment they would rather be drinking its water than the finest whiskey money could buy.

"We've done it!" Dawn screamed, throwing her arms around the nearest man and kissing his bristle-stubbled cheek. "We've done it!"

"We for sure have!" whooped the recipient, Billy Jack, then realized that such enthusiasm would ruin his image. "I'll bet either them or us drown or get bogged in a quicksand, mind."

"Get 'em out of it and to work, Dustine!" Goodnight ordered through his water-sodden whiskers, pounding his grinning nephew on the back. "The rest of the drive're coming and'll need handling."

The Staked Plains had been crossed, the Pecos River lapped around their hips, but there was still work to do. Gathering the cowhands, including a bright-eyed, wildly happy Dawn, Dusty set half to control the arriving cattle, move those that had watered away from the river and hold them. The other half went back with him to meet the drag. It said much for the self-control of the riders in Mark's party that they had stuck to their posts and continued with the grueling work of keeping the drag moving.

Not until noon did the last of the herd quench its thirst and cross the river. The chuck and bed wagons had arrived and come to the western bank to join the cattle and remuda. Last on the scene were the de Martins, helped over in their wagon by laughing, delighted men. There had been losses during the final rush, but not heavy and still more than sufficient steers remained to fulfill the Army's contract.

"All right!" Dusty told the assembled trail crew. "You've done real well and deserve a rest. So I'm giving you a holiday. Right through to tomorrow at sunup."

"I dearly love a generous, kind-hearted boss," Red Blaze whooped. "Danged if I don't celebrate by having me a bath."

The idea caught on and a steady stream of cowhands left the camp carrying a change of clothing and, if they owned such refinements, towels. Going to the bed wagon, Dawn climbed in. It had been cleared of bed rolls by men wanting clothing or the means to reload their soaked revolvers. So she opened up her war bag with the intention of following Red's suggestion. First, however, she figured to let the men get through. Lying on her blankets, she drifted off to sleep.

Voices woke the girl and she stayed still for a moment until her sleep-dazed senses cleared. Looking out of the wagon, she concluded the time to be late afternoon. Then she rose, listening to what was being said.

"Barbe has gone along the river to bathe, Jacko," came de Martin's cultured tones. "Can you go and ask her to come back?"

"Sure can," agreed the cowhand, sounding just a touch too eager. "Which way did she go?"

"Upstream, among those bushes," de Martin explained. "I'd go myself, but I want to take some photographs."

"Shuckens, I don't mind doing you 'n' Miss Barbe a favor," Jacko protested.

"I can just bet you don't!" Dawn thought as she waited silently. "Not when there's maybe a chance of seeing her taking a bath."

Before lying down to rest, the girl had removed her boots. She slipped on a pair of Indian moccasins, picked up the clothing set out earlier, draped her gunbelt across her right shoulder and left the wagon. Already de Martin was strolling toward the fire and Jacko was going at a fair speed in the direction of the bushes. Dawn darted after the cowhand and he turned as he heard her coming.

"Hey, Jacko," Dawn greeted. "Say, Cap'n Dusty wants to see you."

"What for?"

"I dunno. He said for me to tell you if I saw you."

"Reckon I'd best go and see what he wants," Jacko muttered in a disppointed voice. "If you see Miss Barbe, ask her to come back to help her brother take some pictures."

"I'll do just that," Dawn promised.

Watching the cowhand stalk indignantly back to the camp, Dawn shook her head and let out a long breath. If her actions should be questioned later, she would claim that she had delivered the false message as part of a joke.

One thing was certain to her way of thinking. For a smart big-city feller, de Martin sure showed a bad judgment of human nature in picking Jacko to fetch his sister. If Barbe was still either bathing or dressing, Dawn could not see the cowhand acting polite and warning the unsuspecting girl of his presence.

"I'm damned if I know why I'm bothering," Dawn mused. "Only it don't seem right for him to be watching her."

Finding a path, Dawn followed it. She made no attempt to walk quietly, not wanting to startle the other girl by an unannounced appearance. Hearing a frightened feminine cry, she sprang between two bushes and skidded to a halt at the sight that confronted her.

Barbe stood on the other side of a sandy clearing, clad in a flimsy silk shift over the briefest, most daring underclothing Dawn had ever seen. Not that the shift offered anything but the scantiest concealment. Its hem had become spiked on the branches of a bush and was drawn high enough to expose her bare, very shapely legs to the tops of the thighs.

"I—I'm caught. Can you help m——?" Barbe began, making ineffectual attempts to free herself. Then she looked up at Dawn and puzzled annoyance creased her beautiful face. "It's you!"

Maybe Dawn was a country-raised girl, with no more formal schooling than her mother had been able to supply, but she possessed her fair share of natural intelligence. Taking in the scene, she drew some rapid conclusions and did not care for them. Everything about Barbe's attitude hinted that she had been expecting some other person to come on to the scene.

"Just who the hell did you think it'd be?" Dawn demanded, dropping her clean clothes and crossing the clearing to drape her gunbelt over the top of the bush which trapped the other girl. "Let me help you get loose."

Gripping the hem of the shift, Dawn tugged it free from the bush and ripped the material. With an angry hiss, Barbe started to pull away from the other girl and added further damage to her garment. Staggering back a few paces, Barbe's face twisted into an expression of rage which shocked Dawn.

"You did this on purpose!" Barbe spat out, moving forward and holding out the torn edge of the shift. "You cheap little——"

"Don't start mean-mouthing me, you man-chasing bitch!" Dawn flared back. "Pulling a play like this, you could have—— Hey though! How the hell did you know your brother wouldn't be coming out to fetch you? That fancy skirt didn't hang itself on the branch by accident."

"You mind your own business!" Barbe yelled. "I've had enough of you, the whole stinking bunch of you!"

"Which I can't say I reckon a whole heap on you," Dawn replied and started to turn away. "Get dressed. None of the men'll be coming."

Barbe spat out something in a language which Dawn did not understand, but figured it to be anything except complimentary. Then the dark-haired girl caught the blonde by the arm and jerked her around. Up drove Barbe's right knee, aimed at Dawn's groin. Giving the angry oath had been a mistake on Barbe's part. Always a tomboy and with experience gained in childhood scuffles, Dawn turned half-expecting such an attack. So she continued to swing her body and the knee struck her hip instead of its intended target. The force of its arrival sent the slim girl staggering away and with an effort she retained her balance.

"All right!" Dawn hissed. "If that's how you want it——"

Clearly that was just how Barbe wanted it. Letting out another string of what Dawn assumed to be French profanity, the dark-haired girl flung herself forward. Caught by a stinging slap across the face, Dawn cut loose with both hands to retaliate in kind. Then their fingers sank into hair, tugging and jerking while their feet or knees flailed at the other girl's legs and body.

For a few seconds the girls staggered backward and forward clinging to hair. Gasps, squeals and curses broke from them as each tried to throw the other to the ground but retain her own footing. In the matter of hair-pulling

Dawn had the advantage. Her short-cropped locks offered a less secure gripping area than the long black tresses of her rival.

Feeling her fingers slipping from Dawn's hair, Barbe raked her nails down the other's cheeks and closed her hands on the other's throat. Pure instinct made Dawn release her hold and transfer her fingers to Barbe's neck. Reddish blotches formed where their fingers gouged into flesh, yet neither showed signs of releasing her hold. Guttural, croaking sounds broke from their mouths as the choking grips grew tighter.

Dawn had been surprised at Barbe's unexpected strength, but was still the stronger of the two. Slowly she forced Barbe back, digging her thumbs into the other's throat and bending her rearward. Desperately Barbe released Dawn's neck and clawed wildly at Dawn's wrists. Pain brought a screech from Dawn's lips and she hurled the other girl from her.

For a moment Dawn thought Barbe had had enough. Then the beautiful-faced girl attacked again. Launching themselves at each other, they collided with a sickening force. Without any form of planned attack, they grappled wildly for a grip to bring the other girl down. Locking her wiry arms around Barbe's waist, Dawn tried to crush her. Struggling wildly, the black-haired girl encircled the blonde's neck with her right arm and twisted until she held Dawn in a headlock. With her own arms around Barbe's middle, Dawn could do nothing to prevent herself being trapped. Once again Dawn found herself being choked, but with less chance of reprisal. Nor could she use Barbe's method of effecting an escape. Riding with the trail herd did not allow her to grow long fingernails.

Croaking and gasping, Dawn broke off her bear hug. Her hands roved wildly in an attempt to break the hold. Reaching Barbe's head, Dawn's left hand buried into the hair. Taking a firm hold, she jerked Barbe's head backward and at the same moment kicked the other hard behind her right knee. Braced on still legs, Barbe was thrown off balance when her leg suddenly bent forward.

Before she could recover, Dawn had jerked free and they both sprawled in a heap on the sand.

With barely a pause the girls began to roll over and over. It was a wild, mindless tangle in which fists, flat palms, knees, feet, heads and teeth were used indiscriminately. Dawn's shirt ripped down the back and flapped free of her levis, while Barbe's scanty clothing—even less suitable for such treatment—suffered even greater damage. The shift hung in tatters, while the bodice of her underclothes had ripped to bare her torso.

Exhaustion rather than modesty or shame at her behavior made Barbe try to end the fight. How it happened was impossible to decide, but in some way they had each obtained a head scissors on the other. With legs locked about the other's head, they rolled four times and then came apart. Sobbing for breath, Barbe tried to crawl away. Dawn lurched to her feet and flung herself forward. Taking a double handful of the black hair, she dragged Barbe upright. Then she released the girl and swung a punch. Hard knuckles crashed into Barbe's nose and she stumbled backward with hands going to the source of the pain.

"My face!" Barbe screamed, going to her knees. Through the tears of pain which misted her vision, she saw Dawn approaching. "No! No! Don't hit me again!"

Slowly a feeling of revulsion filled the blonde, bringing her to a halt. Yet she wanted to give Barbe a warning to prevent a further recurrence of the flirting which had caused Vern and Willock's deaths.

"All right!" Dawn said, breathing hard and standing over the crouching girl. "What the hell kind of game are you playing at?"

"Do-don't hit me again!" Barbe whined. "Don't hit me and I'll tell you everyth——"

The flat crack of a light-caliber revolver chopped off her words. Struck in the head by a bullet, Barbe pitched sideways. Exhausted by the fight, Dawn reacted sluggishly. For a moment she stood and stared with unbelieving eyes at the other girl's spasmodically jerking body. A soft thud nearby brought Dawn's head around and she saw her Cooper revolver lying on the sand, smoke curling from its muzzle. Faintly she heard shouts and the sound of running feet coming her way. Without thinking, she bent over and picked up the revolver.

Still too dazed to realize fully what she was doing, Dawn turned with the smoking Cooper in her hand. She stood holding the gun, looking in exhausted incomprehension at Barbe's body when the first of the men from the camp burst into the clearing. Everything seemed to be whirling around before Dawn's eyes. Then as her legs buckled under her, she heard a voice from what seemed a long way off.

"My God! She's murdered my sister!"

CHAPTER FIFTEEN
She Has to Stand Trial

Attracted by the sound of the shot, Dusty Fog led the rush
of men to investigate its cause. Bursting through the
bushes, he came to a halt and stared at the scene that met
his eyes. Behind him, the trail hands also stopped and
were shocked to silence by what they saw. Dusty knew the
shock would not last. Even before de Martin came
shoving through the rear of the party, the small Texan
knew he faced a delicate and dangerous situation. Angry,
startled comments rose from the other men as the
photographer made his accusation. Even as Dawn
collapsed alongside Barbe, Dusty swung around.

"Back off, all of you!" Dusty ordered and his eyes went
to the big shape of the cook. "Rowdy, see if there's
anything you can do."

Coming prepared to deal with any kind of trouble—
although not of the type they found on arrival—all the
trail hands held guns. So did Dusty. Yet it was not the
threat of the long-barreled Army Colt in his left hand
which caused the men to obey. At such a time they needed

a leader to guide them and Dusty was that man.

Although the majority of the group obeyed, de Martin ran toward his sister and Josh Narth went to Dawn. Dusty raised no objections, knowing they showed a natural and understandable concern for the girls' welfare. Holstering his Colt, Dusty watched the men do the same. Shock, horror, disbelief and lack of comprehension showed on the tanned faces which Dusty had come to know so well. Staring fixedly at where Rowdy bent over Barbe, Jacko muttered under his breath.

The cook's examination of the black-haired girl did not take long. Looking at de Martin, Rowdy said gently, "There's nothing I can do for her."

"Lord!" the photographer moaned. "Why did it happen? Why? Why?" Then he flung himself to his sister's side and started to sob with his head buried against her naked bosom.

"Dawn's just swooned," Rowdy said after looking at the slim girl. "We'd best have her took back to camp, Cap'n Dusty."

"When I've looked around," Dusty replied. "Do what you can for her here."

"What the hell started them fighting, Dusty?" Mark asked, moving to his *amigo*'s side.

"That's what we're going to have to find out," Dusty replied. "It looks straightforward enough, but——"

"Yeah?" Mark prompted.

Before Dusty could reply, de Martin looked up. Grief twisted at his face and his eyes were red with tears. Slowly he raised a hand to point at where Narth had propped Dawn in a sitting position against his knee.

"What are you going to do about her, Dusty?"

"How do you mean?" Dusty asked, turning from the men as they holstered their revolvers.

"She murdered my sister——"

"Mister!" Narth growled. "I'm taking it that grieving's what made you say that——"

"It's true!" de Martin answered. "Look at the signs. She must have attacked poor Barbe, beat her and then shot her!"

"Why you——!" Narth began and started to rise but was prevented from doing so by Rowdy catching his right shoulder in a paralyzing grip and holding him down.

An angry growl rose from the trail hands and Jacko moved forward, right hand grabbing at his revolver. Instantly Mark brought out his off-side Colt, throwing down on the cowhand long before Jacko's gun cleared leather.

"Back off, friend," the blond giant advised. "All you can do is make things a damned sight worse."

"You would have tried Burle Willock for shooting her brother!" de Martin went on in a loud voice. "Is she to be treated differently?"

"No!" Dusty stated firmly. "She's not!"

"Damn it, Cap'n Fog!" Narth yelled, struggling futilely against the numbing pressure of the cook's powerful fingers. "You're not——"

"I am!" Dusty insisted and looked over his shoulder. "All of you'd best go back to camp. There's nothing you can do here."

"Come on, boys!" Mark said, dropping his Colt back into leather. "Do what Dusty wants. It'll be for the best."

"Yeah!" agreed old Boiler Benson. "There's nothing we can do here."

Turning, talking quietly among themselves, the men walked away. Last to go was Jacko. For a moment he stood staring at Barbe's body. Then, with a strangled gasp, he swung on his heel and stumbled dazedly after his departing companions.

"Josh. Help Rowdy take Dawn back to camp," Dusty went on, watching the cowhand go. "She's to be kept in the bedwagon until I get back."

"Damn it, Cap'n!" Narth blazed. "If you reckon I'm going to stand by and see her hung——"

"Let's hope it doesn't come to that," Dusty interrupted quietly. "But she has to stand trial, Josh. Uncle Charlie may be away with the Kid, but I'll do everything that he would."

"And Colonel Charlie'd do just what Cap'n Dusty's doing," the cook pointed out, sharing the small Texan's unspoken wish that Goodnight had not ridden out with the Kid to scout the land ahead ready for continuing the drive in the morning. He lifted the girl in his arms. "Come on. You can stay with her."

"Don't try anything *loco* like trying to run out with her, Josh," Dusty warned. "All that'll do is make things even worse."

"I'll mind it," Narth answered quietly and followed Rowdy across the clearing.

"Stay with your sister, Edmond," Dusty told the photographer gently. "There's not much a man can say at a time like this. I'm real sorry——"

"Thank you, Dusty," de Martin replied without raising his head. "Dawn must have hated poor little Barbe to do this."

"Maybe," Dusty replied. "I'll know more about it after I've talked to her."

"Then you don't mean to try her?"

"Yes I do," Dusty corrected, picking up the girl's revolver and looking at how the gunbelt hung over the bush. "Maybe you'd best come with me——"

"And leave her?" de Martin moaned, indicating the body.

"It'd be for the best. I'll have her brought in."

Taking the photographer by the arm, Dusty helped him rise. For a moment de Martin seemed ready to resist. Then he let out a croaking sob and walked away. Dusty was about to follow. Looking down, he decided to cover the body's naked bust and bent to do so. Something caught his eye and he looked closer at the body, studying one of the injuries with extra care. Removing his calfskin vest, Dusty draped it across the naked torso. With that done, he followed and caught up to de Martin. Together they made their way back to the camp.

The change in the atmosphere struck Dusty immediately on his arrival. Up to the sound of the shot disturbing them, the crew had been a happy, contented whole. Now tension twanged the air like a snapped bowstring as the trail hands formed groups who sat or stood conversing in low tones. Surrounded by Willock's cronies and others of the Mineral Wells men, Jacko scowled at the bed wagon with savage concentration. Leaving Dusty, de Martin went slowly in the direction of his wagon. Coming to his feet, Jacko walked over to the photographer's side.

"Mark!" Dusty said as the big blond approached him. "I want you to go out to the clearing and stay there."

"Sure."

"Take Pick Visscher with you. Both of you stay there until I send somebody to relieve you. You're to let nobody—and I mean *nobody*—touch *anything* out there."

"Yo! I'll take out a tarp and cover the body."

"Sure. But don't move or touch anything."

"It's done," Mark promised and went to the Mineral Wells men. They showed some surprise at his words, but the stocky Lazy F cowhand rose without argument and accompanied him.

Walking across to the bed wagon, Dusty felt the uneasy stirrings which warned him of danger. Once again the trail crew faced a split in its membership, for some of the men would be sure to back up Josh Narth in Dawn's defense. Others, especially Jacko's bunch, would remember Willock and be equally insistent that Dawn should face trial. Dusty cursed. In addition to Goodnight and the Kid being away, Ahlén was riding the herd with Sherman, Red and Billy Jack. That deprived him, as had sending Mark to guard the clearing, of possible steadying influences and of men on whom he could rely.

On entering the wagon, Dusty found Dawn recovered sufficiently to be able to talk. Sitting on her bed, she dropped a cloth into a bowl of water and turned her half-washed, frightened face in the small Texan's direction.

"D-Dusty!" Dawn gasped. "I didn't kill her."

"Best tell me what happened then," Dusty replied. "All of it from why you went at each other on."

After listening to the girl's story, from her decision to deliver de Martin's message instead of allowing Jacko to do so up to Barbe's death, Dusty stood up.

Narth looked at the small Texan in a challenging

manner and asked, "You believe her, don't you, Cap'n?"

"Can you be ready to face a hearing in half an hour, Dawn?" Dusty said, ignoring the question.

"Damn it——" Narth started to growl.

"We're only a week at most to Fort Sumner, Cap'n Dusty," Rowdy put in. "Can't it wait until we get there and let the legal law handle it?"

"Some of the crew wouldn't hold for waiting," Dusty warned.

"We could hold them!" Narth stated grimly.

"Not without gunplay," Dusty pointed out. "This drive's too important to ruin when there's a way out."

"Nothing's important enough for you to hang Dawn!" Narth spat back.

"Josh!" Dawn put in quietly. "I told the truth about what happened and I'm ready to face up to whatever comes. I know Dusty'll do the right thing."

"You can count on it," Dusty assured her. "Now stay in the wagon. Get cleaned up and changed. I'll send for you when I'm ready."

Swinging himself to the ground, Dusty looked around the camp. He saw Jacko and the Mineral Wells men gathered around de Martin and walked their way. Glares varying from quizzical or challenging to frankly hostile on Jacko's part, met the small Texan.

"Dawn told her story——" Dusty began.

"Which you have accepted as true!" de Martin interrupted.

"Which I listened to," Dusty corrected. "She reckoned that she heard you asking Jacko here to go fetch your sister back to camp——"

"I did. I wanted Barbe to help me take some photographs."

"Only Dawn allowed that you shouldn't ought to be sending a feller to fetch her when she might still be undressed."

"The idea never entered my head," de Martin protested. "I knew I could trust my sister and Jacko both to behave in a proper manner."

"Dawn acted as she thought was for the best," Dusty replied, seeing the rest of the crew gathering around. "When she arrived, she found your sister dressed kind of skimpy and had got that shift, or whatever it is, tangled up on a branch. Dawn allows that she tore it getting it loose, which riled Barbe and made her jump her."

"My sister wouldn't do such a thing!" de Martin insisted and Jacko rumbled agreement.

"What do you reckon happened then?" Dusty inquired, knowing the trail crew were hanging on to every word he and the photographer said.

"I don't want to say anything prejudicial to Dawn before her trial—if she is given one——"

"She's going to be," Jacko put in grimly. "You can count on that."

"Go on, Edmond," Dusty requested as if the cowhand had not spoken.

"All right, Dusty. You asked me to. From the start Dawn was jealous of my sister. You've all seen how she snubbed and ignored Barbe. Until Barbe came, Dawn was queen of the camp. Only Barbe ended all that. With such a beautiful woman around, the men stopped taking notice of Dawn and she hated Barbe for it. Then she may have blamed my sister for her brother's death. So when she heard Jacko and I talking, she saw a chance to take her revenge. She lied to Jacko to send him away, went to where my sister was alone, unprotected, vulnerable, and attacked her."

"Your sister put up a hell of a fight for a lady," Dusty commented.

"Fear and desperation must have lent her strength," de Martin answered. "She fought back with such fury that Dawn was afraid of being beaten, so pulled the gun and shot her."

"And that's how you reckon it happened?" Dusty asked.

"There's no other way——"

"Unless Dawn told the truth. She hung her gunbelt over the bush——"

"Doubtless thinking that she could easily thrash Barbe without needing it," de Martin countered.

"The holster was on the side of the bush away from the clearing," Dusty pointed out. "Dawn'd've had trouble getting to it in a hurry. And she allows that somebody else shot Barbe, then threw the gun over the bushes and she picked it up."

"Is that likely?" de Martin demanded, directing his words to the assembled men. "Who else but Dawn had reason to want my sister dead?"

"Nobody!" Jackos stated and there was a general rumble of agreement.

"Can you prove any of what you have told us, Dusty?" de Martin went on.

"There was no sign on the ground, but the sand'd been churned up in the fussing," Dusty replied. "There was some sand on the gun."

"Gathered when she dropped it and collapsed," de Martin suggested.

"Seems like you're tolerable set on making out Dawn didn't do it, Cap'n Fog," Jacko growled. "I don't mind there being all this talk when Burle Willock shot Vern Sutherland."

"Perhaps Dusty doesn't think my sister's death should be treated in the same manner as the killing of Dawn's brother," de Martin went on.

Angry murmurs rose from the assembled men, deep and menacing as the first rolling thunder-claps heralding the coming of a storm. Then Dusty spoke and his words brought silence in their wake.

"When you talk about your 'sister,' Edmond, don't you really mean your wife?"

Although the small Texan's comment clearly shocked de Martin, he recovered fast. After a brief flicker of shock and surprise, the photographer's face took on a puzzled expression.

"I don't——" he began.

"It's no good, de Martin!" Dusty interrupted. "I saw the photograph in that book. Remember?"

"Yes. But I explained——"

"That's how I know," Dusty stated. "If you and Barbe had been brother and sister, you'd not have bothered. But if you were man and wife, you'd not want me thinking so. I didn't cotton on to it at the time, or until today in fact."

"Why today?" de Martin asked in a brittle voice.

"You put your love-bites where they shouldn't've been seen," Dusty explained. "Only you didn't count on her getting herself stripped to the waist."

"Dawn could have bitten her in the fight!" de Martin spat out.

"And did. Only the other bites'd been done a heap earlier," Dusty replied. "Anyways, there's an easy enough way to prove what I've said. Go find that book with the photographs in it, Solly."

One of the older, more mature Mineral Wells hands, Solly Sodak was all too aware of the danger in the situation. Wanting to help avert trouble, he nodded and moved to obey.

"Here, Solly," de Martin said, reaching into the off-side pocket of his jacket. "I'll give you the key."

While speaking, the photographer grasped something in the pocket and twisted up the side of the jacket to point it in Dusty's direction. Thrusting himself aside, the small Texan missed death by inches. Flame spurted from the front of de Martin's pocket and a bullet fanned hot breath by Dusty's cheek in passing. Across flashed Dusty's left hand, moving as soon as he began to step away from the danger. The right side Army Colt left its contored holster and bellowed on the heels of the crack which sounded from de Martin's pocket. Shock and disbelief twisted at the photographer's face as lead ploughed into his chest. He reeled under the impact, bringing his hand into sight holding a smoking Remington Double Derringer. Fortunately for him, he dropped the weapon as he tumbled backward.

"H-how—how did you——" de Martin gasped as Dusty came toward him.

"I've known that you were carrying that stingy gun ever since you started doing it the morning after Heenan died," the small Texan replied.

"What the hell's going on?" croaked Jacko, staring from Dusty to de Martin and back.

"You mind how we've been expecting that Hayden feller to make fuss for us since the drive started?" Dusty asked and nodded in the photographer's direction. "This's who he sent to do it. Him and his wife." Then Dusty turned his eyes to where Rowdy, Dawn and Narth were running from the bed wagon. "See what you can do for him, Rowdy."

Night had come and de Martin lay on the comfortable bed in his wagon. Looking at the men and girl gathered by him, he read their thoughts which gave added confirmation to his belief that death was close to him. Rowdy had done everything possible, but knew it to be only a matter of time before the end came. So the cook had raised no objections when de Martin asked to see Dawn, Dusty and Jacko.

"You're a smart bastard, Dusty Fog," de Martin said admiringly. "Nobody else suspected me."

"I'd been starting to after you sent Heenan to stompede the herd that night," Dawn objected.

Irritation showed on the dying man's face and he spoke indignantly. "I don't mind you thinking I'm a no-good murdering son-of-a-bitch, Dawn. But I'd hate for you to think I'd be stupid enough to make a fool play like that."

"You're saying that Heenan acted on his own, huh?" the girl asked.

"With a little prompting from my dear, stupid wife," de Martin agreed. "I'm sorry, Jacko. But I knew her far better than you ever could."

"Damn you!" Jacko spat out. "You killed her!"

"Yes. She was so scared of Dawn that she was about to tell what she'd been sent to do. I had to shut her mouth, so did it in a way that might let me earn my fee for wrecking the trail drive."

"By getting us fighting among ourselves, same's you've been trying all along," Dusty guessed.

"It was a technique I developed in the last year of the War to create dissent among various Southern outfits and have used to some success in the East since then. So I thought that it would work with no trouble, especially when I learned that several different ranches were involved. I felt that the interoutfit rivalry could easily be fanned into open conflict. What I didn't take into consideration was the high quality of leadership Colonel Goodnight and you showed, Dusty. That was a smart move at the start, having Mark take charge of Barbe. Yours, I presume?"

"Uncle Charlie's, but I'd likely've done the same."

"I don't doubt it. The scheme nearly worked better than you expected. My dear wife had the morals of an alley cat. She was falling in love with Mark, or as near love as her cashbox mind could conceive. Her simple little brain got the notion that marriage to a rich rancher's son might be preferable to that with a professional trouble-maker. Fortunately I knew how to handle her. She yearned to have her love handed out roughly——I'm sorry, Dawn. This is hardly for your ears."

"I'll live through it," the girl answered, blushing a little.

"Let us say that I persuaded her to remain as she was," de Martin said. "So she met Mark with the reason I had taught her and I hovered in the background. If she had failed me, or offered to betray me, I'd have killed them both and been the tragic brother who found his sister being raped, then shot her by mistake along with her attacker. Mark had a narrow escape that night."

"So did you," Dusty told him. "The Kid was watching you watching them. I'll give you one thing though. At that time we figured the way you wanted us to and hadn't got round to suspecting you."

"I'm good at my work," de Martin stated. "And who'd suspect a man involved in a business like photography? Anyway, I set Barbe to work on the younger hands. She worked on Vern and Burle and in the end caused the fatal fight. Only you stopped the trouble, Dusty——"

"And Heenan killed Burle so we'd not learn he gave Burle the whiskey."

"As soon as he saw Burle show signs of surrendering," de Martin agreed. "I'd arranged for that when I supplied Heenan with the whiskey. You smoothed off the trouble I hoped to start over the crossing of the Staked Plains. Lord, how I had to work to keep Barbe from breaking down during the rains and across the desert. I had promised her we'd have our business done before we needed to cross. You spoiled that. I was willing to settle for tricking Austin into something that would stampede the herd, but you stopped him."

"He'd refused before I cut in," Dusty corrected.

"Be that as it may, the idea failed. So Heenan decided to act on his own. If I'd have been stupid enough to plan that try, I'd certainly not have let you find me in the wagon. Barbe wanted convincing about the crossing and I was doing it when you came back. I hoped to do something on the desert, but Barbe wouldn't let me out of her sight. I think Dawn saw one hysterical outburst——"

"Sure," the girl confirmed.

"Anyway," de Martin continued. "We crossed and on reaching the Pecos I put another scheme into action. I sent Barbe off into the bushes with instructions on what to do. Then I asked Jacko to collect her. The idea was that I should see Austin and express worries about having seen Jacko sneaking off in the direction Barbe had gone to bathe. Naturally Austin would have investigated, to find Barbe struggling to 'protect her honor' from Jacko, having enticed him into a position where she could do so."

"Only I went, not Jacko," Dawn said.

"Seeing Jacko coming after me handed me a hell of a shock," de Martin replied. "When he told me why, I wondered if you'd become suspicious. So I followed and watched the fight. I must say that I was pleased at the thrashing you gave Barbe. I also saw a way of getting rid of her. She was getting a little too unstable for our kind of work. When she looked like blabbing, I picked up your gun from its holster and shot her. Then I tossed the gun near you, waited until you had picked it up, slipped away and joined on to the rear of the men coming from camp."

"She was your wife!" Dawn gasped.

"Not a very satisfactory one," de Martin answered. "I saw a way to get rid of her without the risk of a legal comeback and to finish my work. With Barbe dead, I

knew I could stir up bad feelings. Jacko and some of
Willock's friends, pointed the right way, would demand
that 'justice' was done. There would be others just as
determined that they must protect Dawn."

"You came close to doing it," Dusty said.

"Not close enough," de Martin objected weakly.
"Otherwise I wouldn't be laying here."

"Why've you told us all this?" Dusty asked.

"Why am I betraying my employer, you mean?" de
Martin sighed. "It's simple enough. I've the greatest
admiration for you, Dusty. You've licked me all the way
along the line——And I'd hate like hell to die without
figuring you'll take care of the man who caused me to be
killed."

CHAPTER SIXTEEN

It Licks Being Hung as a Cow Thief

"John Chisum's coming, Colonel Charlie!" the Ysabel
Kid announced, entering the Yellow Stripe saloon where
Goodnight sat with his trail hands waiting to start the
evening's festivities.

It was the second day after the drive's arrival at Fort
Sumner. The Army's cattle buyer had expressed his
complete satisfaction with the three thousand, three
hundred and twenty-eight steers which had survived the
journey from Young County. In addition to purchasing
the whole herd at the promised eight cents a pound on the
hoof, Colonel Hunter had agreed that Goodnight had
fulfilled the contract made on the rancher's last visit.
Buffalo had not been sold, the crew refused to part with
him.

Dusty and Dawn had stayed with de Martin until he
died. During the hour or so he had lingered, the man
cleared up everything which puzzled them; including how
he simulated such grief at Barbe's death. While burying
his face against his dead wife's body, he had rubbed sand

into his eyes and achieved the desired effect. He had also signed a statement which implicated Hayden as his employer.

After de Martin's death, the remainder of the trip had gone by without incident. Receiving payment for the herd, Goodnight had paid out to his crew more money than most of them had ever seen. It would be a long time before the town of Fort Sumner forgot the celebrations which followed.

Coming to his feet, the rancher looked at Dusty and Mark. All around the room, the trail hands moved toward their leaders with hands loosening revolvers in holsters.

"Let's go see him!" Austin Hoffman suggested.

"Hold it!" Goodnight barked, halting the concerted movement toward the batwing doors. "John Chisum saved my life, way back. So if he hands over the Mineral Wells cattle, we take them and call it quits."

"That's good enough for us, Colonel Charlie!" Ahlén stated and the others of the various ranches concerned rumbled their agreement. "We'll play it any way you say."

Needing beef urgently to feed the reservation Apaches, Colonel Hunter had split up and dispatched the herd to various agencies as soon as he had completed the purchase. So there was nothing in the Army's big holding corrals to warn John Chisum that he had been beaten to Fort Sumner. Tall, thickset, bald, with coldly calculating eyes which belied the jovial aspect of his face, he dressed like a saddle-tramp and wore no gun. Swinging open the gate of the nearest corral, he rode aside and allowed his men to drive the herd in.

"That's got 'em here!" declared Chisum's tough-looking segundo, watching two of the hands close the gate on the drag of the herd. "I wonder if that second bunch got through the *Kweharehnuh*?"

"I sure hope so," Chisum answered with such sincerity that he might have been telling the truth. "Fact being, I hope ole Charlie Goodnight makes it——"

"He has!" the man ejaculated, pointing with a thumb. Turning, Chisum stared to where Goodnight, Dusty, the floating outfit and Ahlén were walking from between two of the houses which stood about fifty yards from the corral. Not all the floating outfit, Chisum noticed, for the Ysabel Kid was absent. If Chisum felt any concern, either by the Kid's absence or Goodnight's presence, he gave no sign of it as he rode to meet the approaching party. Behind him, the hard-faced, well-armed trail hands followed like buffalo-wolves on the heels of their pack leader.

"That's not Targue, the segundo he had in Graham," Dusty remarked to Goodnight. "Nor any of that bunch he had along."

"They're the same kind though," the bearded rancher replied.

"Howdy, Charlie," Chisum greeted. "Well I swan if I ever expected to see you here. How'd you lick us?"

"Could be we passed you on the trail one dark night," Goodnight answered.

"You're joshing me!" Chisum chuckled. "It's good to see you see and right pleasing that you'd come to say 'Howdy' to ole Uncle John after a long drive."

"That's not all we're here for," Goodnight warned. "We've come to take the Mineral Wells cattle off your hands."

"To——" Chisum began, conscious of a stirring among the twenty hardcases—selected for gun skill rather than cattle savvy—at his back. "Now I know you're joshing, Charlie. Even if I'd got them steers along, you've got no right to 'em."

"This's Swede Ahlén, segundo of the Double Two," Goodnight introduced. "He and I've got power-of-attorney notes to take possession of all Bench P, D4S, Lazy F, Flying H and Double Two cattle wherever we find them."

"That's not funny, Charlie——" Chisum began mildly.

"It's strange how different folks see things," Dusty put in, noticing the increased signs of hostility among Chisum's hands and indicating the building from between which his party had appeared. "The Ysabel Kid and those fellers there thought it was."

Muffled, startled exclamations and curses broke from

the Chisum hands as they looked in the required direction. The Ysabel Kid and other men carrying repeating rifles had appeared on the roofs of the buildings. More cowhands, also toting shoulderarms, came from between the houses and formed into an efficient fighting line which covered the Long Rail's riders more than adequately. With sickening certainty the hardcases knew they were licked. At their first hostile move, the rifles by and on the buildings would pour a devastating hail of fire upon them. Although his men showed their alarm, Chisum retained his jovial poise. Yet he remained alert for a chance to escape from the trap in which he found himself.

"You did say that you drove our stock here for us Mr. Chisum," Ahlén drawled, after giving time for the realization of their position to sink into the Long Rail riders' heads. "Now didn't you?"

"We're allowed to pay you five dollars a head for doing it," Goodnight went on.

"Five dollars?" Chisum yelped, aware that each steer would bring upward of sixty dollars at eight cents a pound on the hoof. "I'll b——"

"Look at it this way, Mr. Chisum," Dusty interrupted. "The Army's buyer knows none of the Mineral Wells ranchers have sold you any of their cattle. So Colonel Hunter's going to be mighty suspicious when he finds more than a hundred head from each of those spreads in your herd.

"Five dollars ain't much, Charlie," Chisum groaned, knowing that at least three-quarters of his herd belonged to the ranches Goodnight had named.

."It licks getting hung as a cow thief," Ahlén stated bluntly.

"And it'll give you enough money to pay off your loyal hands," Dusty drawled.

At that moment Chisum almost reached bursting point and lost all control of his carefully held temper. Dusty's words had smashed the bald rancher's last hope of goading the Long Rail crew into fighting. Faced with the threat of losing their pay, they might have taken a chance of going against the rifles. Without that inducement, they would be only willing to let things ride. Rage seethed and boiled inside Chisum, but he struggled to fight it down.

"I sure admired to've brought your cattle for you, Swede," Chisum gritted in a feeble attempt to sound his usual jovial self.

"Figured you would be, when you saw it our way," Goodnight said. "Colonel Hunter's on his way here. So I'll pay off your boys and let them go get a hard-earned drink or three. My crew've quenched their thirsts and they'll tend to things from now on."

"One thing, you Long Rail gents," Dusty put in. "The town marshal's appointed Mark, the Kid and me as deputies. We don't mind what fun you have as long as you keep it as fun. Understand?"

"Just in case you don't know us," Mark went on. "I'm Mark Counter and this's Dusty Fog."

"We'll mind what you say, Cap'n Fog," Chisum's segundo promised.

So departed Chisum's last faint hope of turning the tables on Goodnight. With money in their pockets, his hold on the hardcases disintegrated. Burning with frustrated fury, he watched the men paid off and depart, then stood by while Hunter and Goodnight carried out the formalities for the sale of the herd.

"Where's Hayden, Mr. Chisum?" Dusty asked as they gathered in the Golden Stripe saloon waiting for Goodnight to bring the other rancher's money. "You know, the feller who paid you to pull the game on Uncle Charlie, and who you took on to drive for at Throckmorton?"

"I don't know," Chisum replied. "As soon as I figured he was working——"

"Maybe I believe in fairies and Father Christmas, Mr. Chisum," Dusty cut in coldly. "But I've stopped believing in a whole lot of other things."

"We figured that nobody could handle three thousand ' head in one herd," Chisum said, only his eyes showing the hatred he felt for the small, soft-spoken young Texan. "Split the herd into his stuff and them I'd brought. I went ahead, with Hayden following a mite to the north. Up between the Clear Fork of the Brazos and the Pecos we only just managed to sneak by a big band of *Kweharehnuh*."

"And Hayden didn't——" Mark Counter suggested as he and the Kid listened to the conversation.

"I couldn't say."

"Didn't you try to find out, Mr. Chisum?" inquired the Kid.

"Hell no! Them danged Injuns—sorry, Kid—them *Kweharehnuh* was thicker'n fleas on a hound-dawg. I'd got my own men to think about and couldn't risk lives sending to see what might be happening to Hayden's herd. I sure hope they come through all right."

"I just bet you do," drawled the Kid.

The conversation lapsed and Chisum stood moodily staring around the room. No pleasure filled him at the scenes of celebration and merriment. Nor did his feeling of frustration lessen when Goodnight came over with the balance of the money for the herd. It made a pitifully small pile when compared with the amount the bearded rancher had received and which Chisum had fondly hoped would come his way.

Taking the money, Chisum stalked with what dignity he could muster across the room. With his head full of thoughts on how he might avoid a repetition of his misfortunes—the simple way of not taking other people's stock never occurred to him—he failed to see the batwing doors open and three men enter to block his path.

"So you made it, Chisum!" said a cold, angry voice.

Jolted from his considerations of how he might use power-of-attorney notes to his own advantage,* Chisum stared at the three figures before him. Dirty, disheveled and hard-travelled they might be, but Chisum recognized them. Hayden no longer looked dapper, with his torn, filthy clothes and haggard face unshaven. Flanking him, big, burly Targue and Scabee looked mean as all hell. A bloody bandage encased the latter's head and did little to

---

*Chisum's solution is told fully in *Slaughter's Way*.

make him appear any pleasanter. While the two hardcases wore belt guns, their hands were empty. Hayden held a Henry rifle before him and his forefinger entered its triggerguard as he addressed the bald rancher.

"Joe!" Chisum yelled. "Joe Hayden! Thank the merciful Lord that you got through."

"It's no thanks to you that we did!" Hayden snarled. "Why in hell didn't you send back word to us about those Indians?"

Silence fell on the room and every eye turned toward the door. Slowly the customers and staff inched into positions which would allow them to take cover hurriedly in case of gunplay. Chisum was sickeningly aware that he did not have a man in the room whom he might call "friend." Not even Charles Goodnight, for the rancher had made it clear when handing over the money that he considered his debt paid in full. Maybe Chisum did not wear a gun, but cowardice had never been one of his many vices. So he showed no fear and prepared to play the game out to the tricky end.

"I did send!" Chisum declared in tones of sincerity, well-simulated shock crossing his face. "You mean that he didn't get to you?"

"You know damned well 'he' didn't!" Targue spat out. "You let the *Kweharehnuh* jump us so's you could push on clear while we fought 'em."

"Now would I do a meanness like that?" Chisum wailed. "Lord, those words grieve me. Here I've been a-pining and sorrowing at the thought——"

"Of how you'd spend the money you'd get for my herd!" Hayden snarled. "Chisum, when I found out what you'd done on us, I swore I'd find you and kill you."

Having helped fight off the *Kweharehnuh* raiders until rescued by an Army patrol, Hayden and his two men had set out after Chisum. They had lost their herd and wanted to get a share in the money for the bunch the bald rancher drove. Picking up his trail, they had read the story of his desertion and their purpose had changed to one of vengeance. Although Hayden had planned a more subtle way of dealing with Chisum, being confronted by the rancher holding money which must have come from selling the herd drove all thoughts of his plan from his head.

"I—I'm not wearing a gun!" Chisum announced.

"Nobody'll hold that against me when they learn why I killed you!" Hayden spat back.

And the damnable part, to Chisum's way of thinking, was that the other spoke the truth. Once told of his desertion, no western jury would convict Hayden for taking such extreme revenge. Something of an expert in killers, Chisum knew from the expression on Hayden's face that the man intended to carry out his threat. For once—and what might be the last time—the bald rancher's charm and smooth tongue had failed him. Given time, he might have been able to talk Hayden out of the murderous mood——only he doubted if the required time would be granted to him.

"Mr. Hayden!" Chisum heard somebody say and Dusty Fog's voice had never sounded so pleasant to the rancher's ears.

Turning his head slightly, Hayden glared angrily at the three young men who came toward him. While he failed to recognize Dusty, Mark or the Kid, his companions rapidly and correctly identified all three of the Texans.

"Well?" Hayden demanded.

"I've business with you," Dusty stated while the Kid at his left and Mark on his right allowed him to do the talking.

"Make it later," Hayden ordered. "I don't know you."

Taking advantage of the interruption, Chisum began to edge away from the men at the door and clear of the three Texans. He had learned enough since his arrival to figure why Dusty had intervened and meant to make the most of the chance presented to him.

"No," Dusty agreed, coming to a halt and conscious of Chisum's actions. "You don't know me, but we had a mutual acquaintance. De Martin he called himself, but you'd know him better as Soskice."

Shock jolted Hayden's attention from the bald rancher to the small Texan. While he did not know what his visitor

at the Throckmorton hotel had planned to call himself
while working against Goodnight, the man's name had
been Soskice. Mastering his surprise, Hayden gave a
disinterested shrug.

"I've never heard of either of 'em."

"He'd heard of you," Dusty said. "Fact being, he took
an oath on his deathbed that you'd paid him to make
trouble and bust up Colonel Goodnight's trail drive. I
don't reckon he lied."

"He sure as hell didn't!" Chisum screeched, estimating
that he was in a position from which he could safely start
things popping. As he spoke, he flung himself toward the
nearest customers and caused a hurried scattering among
them.

"Damn you, Chisum!" Hayden screamed and started
to swing the Henry's barrel in the rancher's direction.

On either side of Hayden, Targue and Scabee sent
hands fanning down to their revolvers. No less promptly
the floating outfit went into action. Ahead of all the
others, before the Henry completed its turn and spoke,
Dusty's matched Colts roared. He shot at Hayden. Not to
save Chisum, but to prevent the financier from commit-
ting wholesale murder. In his crazed condition, Hayden
would have sprayed the Henry's magazine around the
room without regard for who or what he hit. So Dusty
sent his bullets the only way possible under the
circumstances. Both of them drove into Hayden's head
spinning him through the batwing door with the rifle
unfired and dropping from his hands.

A split second later, Mark's revolvers echoed the
double crash. Caught in the chest by the lead from the
blond giant's guns, Targue pitched backwards to collide
with wall then tumble lifeless to the floor.

Neither the Kid nor Scabee could count themselves in
the class of gun skill shown by Dusty and Mark. While
their hands closed on the waiting guns' butts simultane-
ously, the Kid's old Dragoon cleared leather and spoke
first by a slight margin. Slight, maybe, but it proved just
fast enough to save Dusty's life. Out of a sense of
self-preservation, Scabee had selected the small Texan for

his target. The sledgehammer impact of the Dragoon came while the hardcase was still squeezing off his trigger. Knocked sprawling by the force of the blow, Scabee fired with his gun out of line. Passing between Mark and Dusty, the bullet ended its flight among the bottles behind the bar. Torn open by the round, soft lead ball, Scabee collapsed on to Targue's body.

"You saved my life, Cap'n Fog!" Chisum gasped and his gratitude was not entirely assumed.

"Saved you hell!" Dusty spat back and, thick-skinned though he was, the rancher writhed under the icy contempt in the small Texan's voice. "They could have killed you by inches for all I cared. I was thinking of two young cowhands who didn't finish the drive. But for Vern Sutherland and Burle Willock, I wouldn't've lifted a finger against Hayden until he was through with you."

CHAPTER SEVENTEEN

Goodnight's Dream

And so one of the earliest large trail drives ended, paving the way for Goodnight's dream to come true. On their return to Texas, the trail crew used their knowledge to organize and carry out other shipments. Word of Goodnight's success passed across the Texas ranges, along with his belief in the possibility of a market at the Kansas railroad towns. In the years which followed, almost a quarter of a million longhorns walked the trail carved by the Swinging G to Fort Sumner. More than double that number went north to Kansas and further herds spread across the western plains. The money brought in by the longhorn herds helped the Lone Star State to throw off the poverty and desolation left by the War. Truly it could be said that, guided by men of vision like Colonel Charles Goodnight, Texas grew from hide and horn.

Raw, fast-action adventure from one of the world's favorite Western authors
MAX BRAND

0-425-10018-9	GUNMAN'S GOLD	$2.75
0-425-10117-7	THE GAMBLER	$2.75
0-425-10190-8	DAN BARRY'S DAUGHTER	$2.75
0-425-10346-3	RIDERS OF THE SILENCES	$2.75
0-425-10420-6	DEVIL HORSE	$2.75
0-425-10488-5	LOST WOLF	$2.75
0-425-10557-1	THE STRANGER (On Sale January '88)	$2.75
0-425-10636-5	TENDERFOOT (On Sale February '88)	$2.75

writing as Evan Evans

0-515-08582-0	STRANGE COURAGE	$2.75
0-515-08611-8	MONTANA RIDES AGAIN	$2.75
0-515-08692-4	THE BORDER BANDIT	$2.75
0-515-08711-4	SIXGUN LEGACY	$2.75
0-515-08776-9	SMUGGLER'S TRAIL	$2.95
0-515-08759-9	OUTLAW VALLEY	$2.95
0-515-08885-4	THE SONG OF THE WHIP	$2.75

Please send the titles I've checked above. Mail orders to:

BERKLEY PUBLISHING GROUP
390 Murray Hill Pkwy., Dept. B
East Rutherford, NJ 07073

NAME_____

ADDRESS_____

CITY_____

STATE_____ ZIP_____

Please allow 6 weeks for delivery.
Prices are subject to change without notice.

POSTAGE & HANDLING:
$1.00 for one book, $.25 for each
additional. Do not exceed $3.50.

BOOK TOTAL	$_____
SHIPPING & HANDLING	$_____
APPLICABLE SALES TAX (CA, NJ, NY, PA)	$_____
TOTAL AMOUNT DUE	$_____

PAYABLE IN US FUNDS.
(No cash orders accepted.)